TRAVELERS' SHORTS 2

TRAVELERS' SHORTS 2
Tethers

Robert George Reoch

iUniverse, Inc.
New York   Bloomington

Travelers' Shorts 2
Tethers

iUniverse books may be ordered through booksellers or by contacting:

iUniverse
1663 Liberty Drive
Bloomington, IN 47403
www.iuniverse.com
1-800-Authors (1-800-288-4677)

ISBN: 978-1-4502-3372-9 (sc)
ISBN: 978-1-4502-3373-6 (dj)
ISBN: 978-1-4502-3374-3 (ebook)

Library of Congress Control Number: 2010907688

Printed in the United States of America

iUniverse rev. date: 06/07/2010

For my mum and for my mom:

Frances Joyce Reoch

Beverly Jean Booras

and for

Joon

Introduction to Travelers' Shorts 2

REMARKABLE EVENTS have occurred in my life on a regular basis—such as the time a rainbow appeared over the Punch Bowl (National Memorial Cemetery in Hawaii) as a friend and I were paying respects to someone we didn't even know—*on behalf of another friend who asked us to do it for him.* Isn't that an odd request? It's like a friend giving you a dollar to play a slot machine for him while you're in Vegas. Whose luck is it? Whose respect is being paid? The Punch Bowl is a magnificent memorial and well worth the visit, in any case, so we happily made the trek for our friend. As Zachary and I we were leaving, we stopped and turned around for a last look back. Just at that moment, a beautiful rainbow appeared, arching down from the sky. It seemed to land directly over the gravestone of the friend's friend we had just visited, as though shining on a pot of gold. We were duly surprised. It was dramatic and funny at the same time—as are many of my short stories.

"Tethers" is the theme in this new selection of stories. These tales highlight some of the tethers, *or ties,* that bind us to people, places, and things—whether realized, or not. The connections that bind us may be tangible, such as a space walker's safety line, or they may be intangible—an unexpected dream of someone from the past.

Many of my stories are based upon real events, while others are purely fictional. I've lived a varied life and have always had a vivid imagination. Although I'm usually happiest at home, I thrive on getting out seeing the world too!

Make no mistake. ***Travelers' Shorts*** is *not* a travelogue. There are no vacation stories here. The title of these books is more about shorts as in *short* stories. It says to the traveler (or any reader) they can read a few good short stories during travel, and enjoy the destination when they get there, as opposed to taking on a heavy novel that may linger and nag, unfinished. These stories are intended as enjoyable, meaningful ways to pass the time during boring periods of transit by plane, train, boat, or bus. Sometimes you just don't feel like being bogged down with a lengthy tome and you don't want to read trite newsstand nonsense, either. My short stories provide amusement as well as redeeming value with each episode providing a unique, adventuresome escape in itself, as well as imparting a clever message, subtly slipped-in for good measure.

As an added bonus in this book, you will find a "tether," or two, that harkens back to my first book—a fortunate, accidental device, actually—not a ploy. I did not set out to link my two books—it just happened. There is even a sensational connection between two stories within this very book itself—making for an exceptionally tantalizing read.

Speaking of tethers and friends, I am compelled to say hello to one who forever will remain both: I know you're at the other end of that rainbow now, Zach, and you are smiling as I write this. Our connection will always remain as strong as the strongest of friendships has ever been. While there are other wonderful people, places, and things in my life, one tether will never be broken—that of our bond of friendship. With that in mind, *"Feather,"* I dedicate this introduction in memory of you, and of all of our times together. No book has room enough for what you have meant to me.

Love, *"Dove."*

——Robert George Reoch

Contents

Tethers

SETH WAS GETTING USED TO HEARING the same eerie sounds each time the voices spoke to him in his head. The sounds came just before the voices spoke to him, and then again, when they had finished. Raspy synthesized noises, the sounds were like loud whispers in Seth's inner ear. *"SHEK-ROOSH."* It was always the same. Even though he had been startled from the beginning, Seth felt compelled to listen to the sounds and the voices. Lost and terrified, he was floating alone in space and anxious to hear what the voices had to say. They provided comfort at a time when any form of companionship was vital. The sounds and the voices were Seth's only security.

His eyes wandered to the massive Earth below, his thoughts drifting, remembering the last time he had spoken to his wife as he was leaving. "I'll be watching you too," he had said while holding her.

SHEK-ROOSH—"Who is that person?"—*SHEK-ROOSH*

A voice was speaking again.

"What person?" Seth said.

SHEK-ROOSH—"Of whom you are thinking?"—*SHEK-ROOSH*

"You must mean Gwen," Seth said. Whomever the voice belonged to, it understood Seth's thoughts—without his even

1

vocalizing them. Seth chose to respond aloud because it felt more real. The sound of his own voice reminded him he was still alive.

"She's my wife—my life partner," Seth said.

Since losing contact with the space station, Seth was unsure of where he had wound up. Something had gone terribly wrong during his routine inspection outside. Perhaps a piece of hurling space debris had severed his tether. The fifteen-foot cord had been the only thing keeping him attached to the superstructure while the station circled the planet at 9,000 miles per hour. Now, his thoughts were mainly of his wife and child.

SHEK-ROOSH—"How long?"—*SHEK-ROOSH*

"Since college, sixteen years …"

Seth took a few breaths, noticing a difference in the air he was inhaling. It was more like that on Earth than the air he had been breathing aboard the space station. There was no ozone taste to it. He also realized his current artificial environment was entirely transparent with no visible walls, ceiling, or floor. Yet, he could breathe with his face cover off while somehow hovering in his fixed position in outer space. He was alone except for the alien voices communicating with him.

"I was trained not to panic," Seth said.

SHEK-ROOSH— "What prompts you to say that?"—*SHEK-ROOSH*

Seth had somehow anticipated the next question before the voices had even asked it. "I don't know … Weren't you just going to ask me why I wasn't afraid?" He realized he had picked-up one of *their* thoughts before they had intercepted *his* next one.

"I *am* actually … afraid," Seth said. He was hesitant. He and the aliens were still in the process of adjusting their exchanges.

SHEK-ROOSH—"What happened?"—*SHEK-ROOSH*

"I think my tether was cut by space debris." He had not actually seen what had occurred because it had happened so fast. "It must have been pretty sharp to have cut through my line so cleanly, though," he said. "I never felt any tug on it."

Until he let go of a crossbeam, Seth hadn't realized he was no longer connected to the space station. While attempting a short jump from one section to another, he had found himself floating away with his lifeline trailing loose.

SHEK-ROOSH—"Why did you not summon help?"—*SHEK-ROOSH*

"Like I said, I was trained not to panic. I needed to figure out the best way to get the crew's attention without wasting oxygen or losing my cool."

SHEK-ROOSH—"You are climate controlled."—*SHEK-ROOSH*

"My suit is, yes," Seth said. "I was talking about me … me keeping cool … as in *calm*."

There was a brief silence. Seth stared at the Earth, conscious of the planet's movement. He could feel it turning, even though it was not obvious to his eyes.

SHEK-ROOSH—"An opportunity presented to observe."—*SHEK-ROOSH*

Opportunity to observe. Seth thought the words over.

"How long have you been watching?"

SHEK-ROOSH—"In your language, there is no verbal reference for comparative time-related aspects in a multiverse."—*SHEK-ROOSH*

"*Multiverse.*" Seth muttered the word to himself. He was familiar with the concept of multiple universes—the "many worlds" theory. It intrigued him to hear it mentioned just then. No one had ever proved the existence of multiple tandem worlds.

SHEK-ROOSH—"You have meta-universe theories. We offer they are realities."—*SHEK-ROOSH*

Seth was caught off guard. "I'm listening."

SHEK-ROOSH—"In this sequence, while you were outside your artificial environment there was a dimensional collision."—*SHEK-ROOSH*

Seth attempted to grasp the magnitude of what he had just heard. If his interpretation were correct, whomever the voices belonged to were from a separate universe. Science had been on the right track in exploring the concepts of several universes existing in parallel. It seemed he was now stuck the middle of at least two intersecting dimensions, essentially by himself, hanging suspended in space with his broken tether still attached to his suit.

All at once, a wave of sadness came over Seth, taking his mind away from his discourse with the voices. As he hovered over the planet below, he realized his wife and young son were down there, out of his reach. He felt a crushing despair. What would happen to them if he did not make it home? His eyes began filling with tears causing his vision to blur. He dreaded the awful suffering his wife and son would have to endure if they lost him. Seth's chest ached.

SHEK-ROOSH—"They do not know yet."—*SHEK-ROOSH*

"What do you mean?"

SHEK-ROOSH—"No one on Earth knows."—*SHEK-ROOSH*

"Was this just a random collision, or was this planned? Did you cause this?"

SHEK-ROOSH—"It does not matter."—*SHEK-ROOSH*

"Why? What are you trying to say?"

SHEK-ROOSH—"There is much discord."—*SHEK-ROOSH*

Seth thoughts raced as he struggled to come to terms with his situation. His physical body was suspended in a comfortable, reclining position, yet poised facing downward over the Earth. From his quiet bubble, his view was entirely clear and unobscured. Able to turn his head freely, he could see in all directions, eyeing the great non-atmosphere of known and unknown lights. Seth thought about his wife, Gwen, and his son, Joel down on Earth.

"Oh, my God!" Gwen nearly fainted, standing on the backyard deck. Ever since Seth had gone up, she had been following the International Space Station in the nighttime sky, watching for her husband as he went past. The station was but a single white dot among thousands of other bright spots, but it was the only object visibly moving, and was easy to follow. Gwen had been looking up and following it just then, when it disappeared before her eyes. His dot was gone. Surprised, and in a surge of panic and adrenaline, she had become dizzy, nearly passing out. There must be clouds in the way, she thought at first, but she knew better. She knew exactly when and where to look, but she would rather have been mistaken. *Where is my husband, for God's sake?*

They hadn't needed to use their telescope to monitor Seth. In fact, it was easier to watch for him without it. Even Joel could easily spot his dad's "space yacht" on clear nights. At twelve, he had acquired the same fascination with astronomy as his father. Their home, on the shore of Spy Pond, was miles away from the lights of Boston. When unobstructed by clouds, their view of the night sky was exceptionally clear. When there *were* clouds, however, it became a game to track the small white dot between the clouds as they moved. The sky, on this particular evening, was clear and cloudless.

Unnerved, Gwen thought she had seen a small burst of light at the same instant her husband's lab had vanished from its steady orbit. She double-checked her watch to confirm Seth's regular trajectory time.

"What's wrong, Mom?" Joel stepped from the kitchen door to join his mother on the deck. "Don't worry about the geese," he said. "I think the swans scared them. They're just hiding."

Gwen moved off the deck without speaking and Joel followed his mother. They descended the sloping grass, away from the house, several yards down to the pond.

"It's the mute swans, Mom. They're mean … territorial." Joel stayed close to his mother as they walked onto a wooden pier over the water. Joel continued assuring his mother. "Don't worry … the geese will be fine." They stood in silence, feeling the give of the floating platform under their feet. The Canada geese and the aggressive swans were tucked behind the reeds for the night.

"It disappeared," Joel's mother said. She was muttering something, sounding unsure and confused. She peered back at the sky.

"Hey, where is it?" Joel said. He was squinting and looking

up, scanning the familiar star configurations, aware that the space station should have been visible then too.

"You don't see it?" Gwen's voice choked. She hadn't seen the moving dot reappear as she had hoped. Her heart had begun beating rapidly, but she tried not to show her alarm.

"Where did it go?" Joel asked. He sensed something was wrong.

"Let's just go inside," Gwen said. Joel couldn't see his mother's face in the dark, but he could hear something unusual in her voice.

Isolated in space, Seth gazed on the planet, scanning North America for the tail of Cape Cod, trying to find Massachusetts. His home was in Arlington, slightly northwest of Boston, but he soon realized his current position was nearly on the opposite side of the world. Recognizing Africa, his eyes were drawn to bright flashes of light northeast of the continent. The activity was too intense to be mere lightening and Seth became alarmed by what he was seeing.

South of the Caspian Sea, there were startling bursts of intense light. Seth observed several strobe-like flashes followed by violent explosions immediately above the land's surface. Immense clouds had begun forming over large land areas below the southern shores of the Caspian. Hairs stood up on the back of Seth's neck as he realized what was happening in the Earth's atmosphere below. It appeared as though Iran were under nuclear attack. Nothing else could produce the kind of catastrophic activity Seth was witnessing.

The spectacular trouble on Earth had also drawn the attention of Seth's otherworldly hosts.

SHEK-ROOSH—"A unique opportunity to observe."—*SHEK-ROOSH*

"Is this how you found me?"

SHEK-ROOSH—"Yes."—*SHEK-ROOSH*

"I need to get back! Do they even know I'm gone?"

SHEK-ROOSH—"They know."— *SHEK-ROOSH*

"Who knows?"

SHEK-ROOSH—"There is confusion."—SHEK-ROOSH

"What? Of course, there's confusion! But they must know I'm lost. Can you get me back to the station?"

SHEK-ROOSH—"It was not space debris."—SHEK-ROOSH

Seth's mind raced. His only concern was in getting back to his space station. He was desperate to let his wife and son know he was alive. By now, they must have heard something. His thoughts were jammed with the logistics of getting back inside the station, and about transportation back to Earth.

SHEK-ROOSH—"Situations grow more active below."—SHEK-ROOSH

"What do you mean? What's happening down there?"

SHEK-ROOSH—"After a collision, we observe."—SHEK-ROOSH

Seth was less interested in the visitors' agenda and more worried about his own needs.

"Aren't they looking for me? How are they going to find me with you holding me here?"

SHEK-ROOSH—"We intercepted you drifting."

"I realize that and I'd like to shake your hands and thank you, but I can't even see you. Where are you?"

SHEK-ROOSH—"There was an interaction between proximate realms."—SHEK- ROOSH

"Realms?" Seth was trying his best to understand.

SHEK-ROOSH—"Worlds."—SHEK- ROOSH

The voices stopped for a moment and Seth sensed he needed to listen and try to calm himself.

SHEK-ROOSH—"The attachment to your ship was severed as we crossed into your realm—the consequence of an event."—SHEK-ROOSH

"What event?"

SHEK-ROOSH—"Bubbles merged."—SHEK-ROOSH

"Bubbles?"

Seth's understanding of bubble theories and meta-universes was limited. He had never seriously pondered the possibilities of separate worlds actually colliding. He could never have imagined being part of an accident such as two universes converging like soap bubbles in a giant bathtub.

"We merged like bubbles. Is that what you're saying?"

SHEK-ROOSH—"Correct—a rare occurrence."—SHEK-ROOSH

Seth was overcome by his unrelenting scientific curiosity. He couldn't resist asking more questions despite his urgent circumstances.

"What would have happened if there wasn't a merger?" Seth was curious to know their answer, even though he thought he knew it already. "What if one or both of the bubbles had popped?"

SHEK-ROOSH—"Calculations indicate high probability of measurable destruction."—SHEK-ROOSH

"Are you stranded here?" Seth hadn't intended to ask the question. It just came out.

SHEK-ROOSH—"Our travel capability is intact."—SHEK-ROOSH

Seth closed his eyes. He was again feeling a wave of sadness and growing fear. Too much was happening all at once. He wanted to travel back to Earth.

SHEK-ROOSH—"Our tethers remain functional."—SHEK-ROOSH

"Yeah, good for you."

So what if the visitors could go back to where they came from. To where and to what? Seth was tired. As he became wearier, his frantic thoughts began to dwindle and subside. The questions in his mind had taxed his energy. Exhausted and drowsy, he eventually gave-in to fatigue and fell asleep. The Earth continued rotating and exploding while he dozed.…

When he opened his eyes again, Seth noticed his vantage point over the Earth had changed. The planet had made nearly a half turn. His visitors were aware the moment he became conscious again.

SHEK-ROOSH—"Your body required sleep."—SHEK-ROOSH

Seth had slept soundly for nearly forty minutes.

SHEK-ROOSH—"We do not inhabit planets."—SHEK- ROOSH

"You don't huh?" Seth was gradually becoming alert.

Adjusting his focus onto the planet again, he could see the lights of Manhattan. He shifted his line of sight over to Long Island, and followed the coast of New England up to the cape and then west, where he spotted the lights of Boston proper. Gwen and Joel would be at home in Arlington, slightly northwest, in their old Georgian home. Their house has stood for over a hundred years, amidst the trees overlooking Spy Pond. A mastodon tusk had been pulled from the bottom of the water decades before Seth's family moved into the house. The intact prehistoric relic was on display at a museum a short distance down the road from their home. It was on that road, over two-hundred years prior, where the colonial militia of "Minutemen" had fought the British for freedom in the days when Arlington was known by the Indian name, Menotomy, *swift running water.*

Seth knew exactly which times his wife and son would look up to search for his station. They rarely missed watching for the ISS as it passed. It gave Gwen and Joel great comfort to see it. Seth was essential in their universe, just as they mattered most in his world. Seth imagined them looking up, but in fact had no idea of the actual time.

SHEK-ROOSH—"Inhabited planets become hostile environments and die."—*SHEK-ROOSH*

Seth was disturbed by the assessment. "Why are you telling me this? Is there something I should know?"

SHEK-ROOSH—"Observe."—*SHEK-ROOSH*

Seth gazed down and focused on the small area northwest of Boston, watching in silence and hoping Gwen and Joel were safe. After several seconds, his eyes were again drawn to more unexpected lights. Streaks of amber light had begun appearing over western portions of North America. Multiple glowing objects were traveling in a steady trajectory over Montana, North Dakota, and Wyoming. Seth knew there were rocket silos in those areas where were housed the Minuteman missiles.

"My *God.*" A chill ran through Seth. "They've gone DEFCON."

SHEK-ROOSH—"It was not space debris."—*SHEK-ROOSH*

"What do you mean? Of course it's not space debris!" Seth was confused and agitated. He didn't realize the voices weren't speaking about the missiles just then. They were speaking again about Seth's separation from the space station.

SHEK-ROOSH—"You did not actually see your tether break."—*SHEK-ROOSH*

"Tether? What? No, I didn't see it."

Seth was uncertain about what had happened. The voices reminded him again.

SHEK-ROOSH—"You did not actually see your tether break."—*SHEK-ROOSH*

"Space debris. It was cut by space debris, right? Or, did you cause this to happen?"

SHEK-ROOSH—"No. It was not space debris."—*SHEK-ROOSH*

Seth realized he had not actually seen anything hit his line. It had happened too fast. He had not even felt a tug on the tether at all—something he would have noticed if a fast moving object had hit his line. One moment he was performing work outside the station; the next, he was hovering over the Earth. The space station was no longer in sight and he was alone except for having become an unwitting guest of extraterrestrials—speaking to him through his mind. Now, warhead-carrying missiles had been launched by the United States.

SHEK-ROOSH—"The station disappeared with the other end of the tether."—*SHEK-ROOSH*

"Wait—*what?* ... Hold on a second." Seth began to recall the images he had seen, just before falling asleep, of explosions over the Middle East. Now he realized it wasn't a dream. "What the hell is going on down there?"

SHEK-ROOSH—"The bombs came from Tbilisi."—*SHEK-ROOSH*

"Tbilisi, Georgia?" *There are Russian missiles there.*

On Earth, Seth's son joined his mother in the kitchen. They had both made the same observation. The space station had disappeared from its orbit and neither of them knew the reason why.

"What happened, Mom?"

"I don't know, but it looks like we are going to find out."

They huddled together and watched an emergency broadcast on the kitchen monitor, as the news commentator spoke.

"In an apparent retaliation for the destruction of the International Space Station by what Russian Federation officials are calling an unprovoked act of aggression by Iran, nuclear missiles have begun detonating over Iran's capital city of Tehran, apparently launched from mobile missile launchers stationed in the former Russian state of Georgia."

"No!" Joel's head jerked as though he'd been hit. He stood rigid next to his mother.

"It's gone," Gwen said. She squeezed her son's shoulder. She knew then, with certainty, her husband wasn't coming home. "They think the Iranians shot it down."

"How?" Joel said. "That's impossible, right?"

"They're saying Iran fired one of those high energy particle beams or something."

"I thought those were only experimental."

"I did too—I don't know, Joel. Who knows what's going on over there?"

Joel could feel his mother shaking.

"Your Dad told me that if something like this were to happen, our country would respond somehow," she said. "They'll have to launch our missiles now and try and stop things from getting worse."

Wrestling away from his mother, Joel ran out the back door to the lawn and looked upward.

Above the planet, Seth listened to the voices in his head.

SHEK-ROOSH—"Your space station ceased to exist after the event."—*SHEK-ROOSH*

The revelation helped Seth begin to make sense of what was happening.

"But, on Earth, that's not what they think happened, is it?" Seth said. "They think the station was blown up deliberately, don't they?"

SHEK-ROOSH—"They misinterpreted reality. Now they are bombing."—SHEK-ROOSH

"I need to get home!"

On Earth, Joel remained standing in the backyard staring at the sky. The late summer morning was dawning balmy and quiet. Soon, children would come marching along the trail, laughing on their way to day camp at the pond.

All at once, the swans and geese took flight out of the reeds in a panic, honking and squawking as they skimmed over the water toward the horizon. Something unseen had frightened them. Near Joel's foot, a squirrel bolted over the lawn and up a tree. Joel's attention was then drawn toward the west.

The sounds were coming from approaching rocket engines. Quickly growing louder, the missiles explained the animals' mass retreat. Three supersonic objects were traversing the blue, each leaving a line of chalk in the sky, each dark spot spraying hot vapor behind it like a fire hose while soaring east. The boom of the sound barrier being shattered shook the air—another shot heard 'round the world.

Seth could only observe the catastrophe escalating on Earth.

SHEK-ROOSH—"We can offer choices."—SHEK-ROOSH

"*What?*" Seth focused intently. "Tell me what you've got. I need to get back home."

SHEK-ROOSH—"To be precise, your choices are limitless."—SHEK-ROOSH

"*Limitless?* What do you mean, *limitless?* That's not precise! That's means *zero* to me. What are you saying?"

The visitors attempted to help Seth understand.

SHEK-ROOSH—"Everything that exists is replicated in infinite alternate universes. Variations of all, including entire sequences of events, occur in other tandem worlds, in each instance, with sometimes infinitesimally small *differences.*"—SHEK-ROOSH

Allowing Seth time to absorb what he had been told, the visitors were silent for a minute before continuing.

SHEK-ROOSH—"You exist in countless incarnations, not merely what you see now. Each existence has a variant from one existence to another. Today, you need only choose one variant and we can place you in that existence."—*SHEK-ROOSH*

"You mean I can change what will happen?"

SHEK-ROOSH—"Yes."—*SHEK-ROOSH*

"I can choose what I want to change?" Seth was beginning to feel hopeful.

SHEK-ROOSH—"Yes. The effect will be significant."—*SHEK-ROOSH*

With hope growing, Seth considered his options. It seemed too good to be true! He concluded that the choice was simple. It was only a matter of avoiding another instance of colliding bubbles.

"Can you place me in a parallel universe—in a series of events—where we don't cross paths? ... Where I won't meet you?"

SHEK-ROOSH—"It can be done."—*SHEK-ROOSH*

"Please do that! I don't want to watch Earth die from here with my wife and child in it."

Seth had no time to reconsider.

SHEK-ROOSH—"It happens now."—*SHEK-ROOSH*

In the next instant, something had changed. Seth was still adrift in space, but something had changed—he could sense it. There was still no sign of the space station. Inside his space suit was complete silence. He then noticed that Earth was no longer in view. Turning in all directions, he was unable to locate the planet. The change was not what he had expected.

"Hello?" He waited, but no response came. There were no voices. "Hello," he said again ... and waited ... with no response.

Seth was completely alone this time. Without having converged with another universe, there were no visitors. Nothing in the universe around him appeared as it had before. The distant planets and stars were now in different positions. He had no bearing on where he was. *This can't be.* A sense of dread and helplessness began taking hold of Seth.

Why am I here? Is anyone listening? His aloneness was quickly becoming unbearable. He needed to hear the voices in his head again, *at least once.* Waves of melancholy washed over him. *Look at me. I'm pathetic.*

Gazing out at blackness dotted with suns and planets, Seth's long white tether trailed away from his suit—its end frayed. His safety line appeared to have been severed by a violent tug.

On Earth, Seth's wife and son watched the news in the kitchen as Gwen tightly clutched Joel close to her. The broadcast anchorwoman explained the tragedy.

"All nine astronauts are believed to have perished in the accident, when an apparent piece of unidentified space debris hit the station, causing instantaneous disintegration. It was determined there was no possibility of survival by any of the crew."

The change, which Seth had asked for, had occurred. There were no colliding universes and thus no voices speaking in his mind. However, in this existence, the variant of space debris did occur.

Seth drifted alone with his thoughts. His only comfort was in knowing that somewhere, at some time, in at least *one* of countless other dimensions, things would be different. He dreamed of still another realm, where he would be living out a full life with his family on another Spy Pond. He and Gwen would finish raising Joel. They would watch him come unto his own and produce grandchildren for Seth to take rowing on the pond. It would be an idyllic life. They would cook outdoors and watch fireworks over the pond with laughing children running in the warm summer.

Seth's only solace came from within his own mind and his own thoughts as he lingered and drifted in space thinking about a possible existence in another dimension, on another plane, in another time. In his immediate reality, however, alone and in the dark, Seth ultimately cried himself quietly to sleep and was lost for the duration of that existence.

SHEK-ROOSH—

The Plane and the Matchbox Car

MISSING, ARE THE TWITCHING noisy junior high boys.
I'll be playing baseball there one day too. This is the only dream
I'm ever going to remember. I'm walking past the chain link fence
and seeing the playing field through it. It's empty—no jocks in
gray sweat pants and gym shorts playing for life or death, and the
non-sports ones faking it. The clay soil of the baseball diamond
is hot from the sun, dry, and devoid of bodies. The grass beyond
is just cut, but I can't smell its raw aroma. It feels nostalgic and
lonely. I still have a year to go.

My presence on the beach goes unnoticed by the sandpipers.
They run amok on their stick legs, too busy poking at the wet sand
on the shore. I'm alone on a bank of warm sand above them, lying
on my stomach on my towel. I open my eyes for a few seconds,
just slightly, and see the tight folds of skin inside the bend in my
elbow. The small blonde hairs on my tanned arm shine like glass
threads in the sun.

The baseball diamond bakes in my dream. There is a low-
flying object coming in. It seems out of place.

On my stomach on my beach towel, half asleep, I stare at my
arm, vaguely realizing I'm dreaming of the baseball field. I'm lying
in warmth. I hear ocean waves reminding me I'm at the beach.

I'm too lost in my half-dream to awaken, yet I'm hazily aware of myself. It's happened before, being held prisoner in my nap—this dream. I have nothing pressing to do. My breathing is fine and I feel no urge to panic. Since I'm not conscious enough to move, I resign myself to remain under, imagining it's by choice.

Approaching the baseball diamond from the air, the object floats slowly above the empty field. A small craft—an airplane—it descends over second base, a sight without sound. From outside the fence, I watch the miniature plane continue its weary, deliberate journey.

At the beach, a cloud lays down a shadow. I feel it on my feet first, and then it goes like a hand smoothing up my legs and my back, raising goose bumps.

Now, the gliding craft is over the pitcher's mound. A small, single-engine warplane, it resembles the type in old films, flown by Japanese. Nearing home plate with no engine noise, my mind wants to invent sounds for it, but my daylight dream has only silence, which I cannot correct. The plane feels out of place, so small and aeronautic. It should be a kiddy ride at a carnival and have its fuselage painted brightly. On the contrary, it is stubbornly colorless. Like the oiled dirt of a carnival field, it is dull and brown. The plane unapologetically presents itself, appearing as a relic from the past, while the baseball diamond receives it in kind, casually underdressed without its white chalk lines.

Lying on the warm sand on my colorful cloth, a quick tickling air runs up my bare back. Little gusts get up the legs of my jams too—quick little surprises—finding sensitive areas. In my towel, I smell suntan lotion where my nose rests. Peeking out again through half-closed eyes and a comb of lashes, I watch the hairs on my arm quiver in the wind. Shore sounds fade and my eyes close again. I doze.

The foreign plane is sinking lower to the ground. Noiselessly, it comes down toward home plate, moving like a dangling marionette, but smoothly and with no sudden hops, only graceful downward dips—descending. Finally, it settles softly on the ground, not raising dust.

The wind kicks up a corner of my towel, covering my nose and eyes. I'm enveloped in laundry aromas and suntan scents. A wave's heavy thud causes my eyes to flutter briefly. I sense the sandpipers out there, somewhere nearby, trotting up and down the water's edge, jabbing at the bubbles in the sand. A seagull cries out a lonely self-talk. The sun is warm again on my back. I wiggle and stop. I dissolve back into the sand, sleeping in my colorful shade.

The cockpit is murky, but there's movement inside. The occupant has dark hair—maybe it's a leather cap. Curiosity compels me to go and meet the man in the airplane. He's slowly gathering himself to get out.

On my long, vacant stretch of beach, I am alone except for the birds. Always deserted, few people know of the place but me. I feel another covert gust for a second, and then slumber again.

I get over the fence without ripping my pants. A short span of grass and I'm to the infield, standing at first base, watching the airplane. The smudged canopy opens upward, arching on its hinge. Someone is getting out.

My secret place on the beach is protected, so I bring little with me and leave nothing behind, never intending to take anything away. The dreams, I can't help.

I walk toward home plate while the small man extracts himself from the fuselage. Over the side he goes, down onto a wing. Then, with an easy jump, he is on the ground on his feet. He appears my size, although slightly bent from sitting. Wearing goggles and a pilot's suit, his face is deeply tanned or sooty—or both.

Inside my towel world, I smell previous beach visits, the ones with friends and ocean water, and hot dogs. I'm darkly tanned and my hair is sun-bleached from long days outside. It is all captured in my towel. I'm still trapped in my dream.

Removing his goggles, pale circles are exposed, ringing dark eyes. He blinks while taking breaths of fresh air and observing his surroundings. Seeing me, sudden interest shows in his surprised eyes. A smile bursts over his face. A joyful grin, it feels familiar and warm. Letting go of his goggles, he jogs toward me laughing. I stop walking and hesitate as he nears.

The clouds above the beach make another pass across my back. I shudder in my nap, still captive, and wait for the sun to warm me again. I slumber.

He rushes into me and hugs me warmly, smelling of engine oil and ozone. His docile eyes are happy—joyous. Tears well up and fall aside, washing away the soot in rivulets down his cheeks. To have found me is of utmost consequence to the man. He is overcome as I merely stand and absorb his ecstatic face and accept his tear-framed smile as delivered.

Another wave thumps the shore with a deep, subhuman sound that I can feel in my stomach where I lie. There's the hush and fizz in its aftermath, and the sound of bubbles being spit out by the sand as the water backs away, the receding foam pulling me deeper into my dream.

Standing in front of me, the man removes a small, blue object from his pocket. There are light scratches in its metallic paint—it's a toy. He holds it out on his palm, gesturing for me to take it. I think I've seen it before, but I can't recall—at first. Then it comes to me. It is a matchbox car with little bite marks in it. He places the small car in my hand while looking into my face. It is a reward for some forgotten deed.

As I doze on the beach, the sand has begun blowing harder, hissing in my hair and getting in my ears. I cannot move.

Now, the man stands at bended arms length, shaking my shoulders gently and smiling still harder. He openly weeps his sad tears of happiness. He is satisfied with his mission. It has been completed as he had hoped. His gratitude pours from his face.

A burst of wind takes the towel from my face. Free of my sensual cover, the sun gives warmth to my face again. I half open my eyes to see my arm hairs still sideways, wiggling. Stubbornly, my dream keeps me fastened to the sand, not letting me go yet.

Somewhere between first base and home, I wanted to fly. Perhaps my friend would allow me a trip in his airship. I'm sure he would permit me to fly it, if asked. He would gladly let me soar over the bay in it at least once. I could fly to Coronado and back. I would be quick. I would promise not to be long and maybe he would agree right away, but no—no, my dream is saying—no.

Men don't always give up their toys so easily—even in dreams. My mirage fading, I knew I would be settling for just the car.

My hand snatched at the air as I opened my eyes in sunlight and realized I was waking. It bothered me not being able to say goodbye to the man who had been so affected by our meeting. I felt a loss, not knowing what had become of him.

Sand blew across my face and my shoulders as I sprawled alone on my towel. I felt something had changed. I sat up and began to brush it all off. Another cloud shadow passed and I forgot about the plane. The sun came out again and I forgot about the toy car. My airplane illusions subsided as my revived eyes went to the ocean. The tide was closing in on my private stretch. Only a few aimless birds remained far down the shoreline. I shook off my towel and left.

The next morning, as I neared the grammar school and heard the buzzer sound, I knew I could still reach my classroom on time. I squeezed between the gate and the fence and began running across the open schoolyard. Light sunburn on my back reminded me of the beach. Others still on the blacktop weren't hurrying to the buildings, so I stopped running. I could take my time. I walked and remembered my dream as I looked down at the playground sand. I was reminded of a recent friend whom I had walked with on the playground.

As I trekked across the sand, I passed behind a wooden backstop and found the blue car sitting on a bench. I stopped at the sight of it and stood eyeing it, dumbstruck. My friend had shown me the very toy only weeks prior while we were walking home for lunch. As each of us had been going to our own homes during lunchtime, we had begun walking together and become friendly over several days. My new friend's life then ended shortly after we met. His tortured mother had come to believe her husband wasn't coming home from the war, having not heard anything for weeks. Unaware of his imminent return, she had only to wait a single day longer. Instead, he returned to find his wife and three children dead in their home, taken by her hand in grief. It was a gun. I picked up the toy car and continued across the sand.

The little scratches in the matchbox car's paint were from my friend's infant sisters. They had been teething on the toy and John had taken it to school to keep it from them. He didn't want them poisoned by the paint. The matchbox car was still in his pocket when he went home at lunchtime, the last time I saw him, I had thought.

Handling the small blue car as I walked, I recalled my dream on the beach. It then made sense.

You're welcome and thank you.

I put the toy in my pocket and kept it.

I stopped looking for my friend while going to and from school, but at times felt anger seeing his empty desk. I moved on.

One gift was enough. There would be other opportunities to fly—but this is the one dream, the only one I remember.

Brake Cake

"HERE YOU GO, TAKE IT."

"No! ... You take it."

"*You* take it, you *diseased toad.*"

"Take it before it gets all mushed! *Hurry.* It's gonna fall on Jesse's head!"

"If either one of you drops that cake, I'm—"

It was the top layer of the wedding cake, untouched and uneaten. Neither Scott nor Kristie wanted it in their laps while mother was driving. I watched from the front passenger seat as they argued in the back seat, and Mom held her breath in the driver's seat.

It had begun to rain heavily just moments after we had all piled in. Already, it was going to be a long drive home. Jesse, the youngest, sat quietly in the middle in the back seat, while Scott and Kristie argued on either side of him.

"*You* hold it." Kristie said. She shoved the cake toward Scott over Jesse's head.

"No. *You* hold it." Scott pulled his hands away and sniggered. The round cake layer was somehow staying on its flimsy paper plate and not sliding off—defying the odds. By rights, Jesse should have been wearing the cake in his hair already.

"*Take* it, you *Hamburglar!*" Kristie shouted.

"Hamburglar!" I laughed. "Hamburglar?

"No! *You* keep it, *snail tracks!*" Scott pushed it back again. "You're not *even* snail tracks. You're a dried up *slug* on the sidewalk!"

"E-e-e-w! That's *gross!*" Kristie tried not to laugh.

"Get it out of my face!" Jesse said. The cake hovered at his nose.

"Give me that cake!" Mom said, leaning inside the rear door. The three were startled. "What is *wrong* with you brats?"

Jesse smiled in his seat between his older siblings. Mom wasn't yelling at him. She just smiled back at him.

"Here, why don't you hold it for me, Jesse?"

"I don't want to!" Jesse folded his arms.

"Fine. Give it to Bobby then," Mom said. She then pulled herself out of the back and returned to the driver's seat.

"Great," I said. "Just give me the stupid thing." I took the cake from Kristie, and placed it in the middle of the front bench seat, between Mom and me. "I just hope it doesn't slide all over the place," I said.

Mom gave me a look that said *you had better hope it doesn't slide around, Buster Brown*. It was going to be a long drive home.

The wedding reception had hardly been worth the trip as far as I was concerned. I had long ago resolved that my older brother, Jimmy, had become a lost cause. He was too far-gone ever to overcome his resistance to authority. It was just wrong how he wore a vest made of fake fur with no shirt, and a skull ring with fake rubies for eyes. It was actually more disappointment that I felt, rather than out-and-out disdain. My brother could be forgiven for his countless misdeeds such as beating up the high school principal, or spitting on old people just for being old, but it was all of his other weird shit that added up to his not fitting into own particular little world order. A hero gone rogue and then dressing so badly just did not click in my mind. How such a perfectly intelligent person could become such a slob was baffling to me. Besides, it wasn't fair that I got acne and Jimmy didn't. I couldn't believe my brother was even getting married.

At least Jimmy had tried dressing up for the occasion. He wore a cardigan sweater with a white shirt and tie for the ceremony. Yet, with his long hair and beard, and his raggedy old jeans hanging halfway down his ass, he still made the perfect anti-establishment groom—but *even then* it made no sense—because he had gotten married at a City Hall in a cheesy civil ceremony. Why bother?

Our delegation of family still living at home did not actually attend the sterile ceremony anyway—which was fine with me. Mom would not take us out of school for a day just to attend a wedding—*so was the excuse she made to Jimmy*. She had other reasons to abstain from going, although none of them had anything to do with school, or even wedding attire.

Mom was not happy about her son's marriage being dispensed in a city she hardly knew. Instead of being married in our former home town of Chula Vista, where Jimmy and his bride were already living, my brother booked a judge in the snarky town next door—the town that people liked to call "Nasty City." Mom made excuses for not going, saying it was only because of school, but that we would all happily drive down for the reception afterward. Thus, we made the long trip from Lakeside to Chula Vista solely to attend the half-assed wedding reception at Jimmy's crappy rented house in our dear hometown of Chula Vista—just one community over from Nasty City.

Mom and my older sisters already disliked the bride. They were convinced she was an undesirable flower child.

"She's a space cadet."

"A tramp."

"She's got a yen for wine."

They swore, too, that Rose—the bride—was probably pregnant. What Jimmy saw in Rose, I could not fathom. Her appearance was that of a waifish ghost. She was Goth before there even *was* Goth. Nobody would ever have described Rose as seeming rosy, either, although she would sometimes smile coyly when someone glanced her way. I noticed she had a sneaky laugh, which I didn't trust. Whenever she whispered secrets to my brother, she would snicker and cover her mouth while her eyes darted around the room, looking to see if anyone were watching. It was creepy the way she came across as both coarse and delicate at the same time.

We didn't have to stay long at the gathering. After the adults had drunk a few glasses of Cold Duck, and I had slammed down a few gulps myself when no one was looking, and after everyone had eaten some crackers and cheese and a small piece of wedding cake, we finally departed the maudlin glad-fest. We had hung around just long enough to have become bored and for Mom to have finagled the top tier of the wedding cake to take home. She was going to keep it in our freezer, following tradition, and save it for the couple's first wedding anniversary. That was just blind optimism. It was just freakin' lovely. It was pathetic. I didn't care, really. All of it was just so much wacked-out misplaced sentiment to me.

"Thank God that's over!" Scott said. At least I hadn't said it. We were back in the car.

He was slumped to one side, his head leaning against his window, mouth gaping. He appeared tired as he squinted to see the rain outside the car in the dark. He was tired from carping about everything all the time, all day long.

"Be careful, Mom, okay?" Kristie said. She went back to her pleading-for-mercy routine in the back seat. With the cake fracas out of the way, she could resume being terrified of Mom's driving. Kristie had white-knuckled the entire drive down from Lakeside that afternoon, expecting some terrible automobile calamity to occur. Now, as we were preparing to drive home again, she was already upset and nearly petrified at the prospect of the return drive. Nearly every time Kristie had been in the car with Mom in the past, something had happened to frighten her. Mom had only recently obtained her license. She had needed to buy a car to get around our sprawling new tract-home neighborhood in

Lakeside. Nothing was close enough to walk except my high school. The younger ones were taking the bus. Everything else required Mom to drive, which had been earning her notoriety with her passengers.

I was aware of Jesse having also been involved in a few of Mom's driving incidents, yet he had never complained, even when Kristie and Scott had been unfavorable witnesses. However, Jesse was too small to see over the dashboard. Therefore, if Mom had run the occasional stop sign or had driven 35 miles per hour on the freeway, only Kristie and Scott had seen enough to fear for their lives. While Kristie developed full-on paranoia and Scott gained more reasons to complain, Jesse remained oblivious and faithful to Mom.

The main reason I was indifferent about Mom's driving, was that I was rarely in the car with her. In fact, when I was in the car I was usually the one driving, and most often I was by myself, although I wasn't legally allowed. I would drive to the market—with permission—even though I was too young for a license. I never asked why I was allowed. I liked to imagine the reason as being Mom's warped vision of pioneer spirit lent of necessity due to our big move to the wilds of tract housing. We were living in wide, spread-out territory. Since nearby conveniences were few, it was easy for me to find plenty of necessary reasons to drive. I was having a blast, driving at such an early age. Boys are practically born with steering wheels in their hands, after all. Nevertheless, I had heard enough about Mom's driving to sympathize with Kristie's fears, so I did my best to stick my nose out of it while she aired her grievances.

"Bobby, why don't you drive?" Kristie suggested.

"Yeah, right," I responded. I had not expected that. She knew I didn't have a license. I was not at all interested in driving just then. Besides, it was much farther to drive from Chula Vista to Lakeside than it was to make a run to the supermarket. Obviously, Kristie was desperate, but I was not yet ready to drive several miles on the freeway in the rain.

"But, you drive to the store all the time!" Kristie said. She was pressing it.

I kept still. Mom was due to blow up at any moment.

"Be quiet, Kristie!" Scott said.

"Bite me, hairball!" Kristie hissed as she opened her car door. We watched her scoot out of the car and stand outside in the rain in protest. After several chaotic minutes of Mom yelling and the rest of us coaxing, Kristie finally got back inside, still nervous, but now soaking wet, as well. Once again, Kristie began pleading not to go. Usually, she was not such a wimp. I found it difficult to understand why she was so terrified of Mom's driving. If I could drive without incident, I was sure our mother could too. Our car was intact. There were no dents or broken side mirrors to show for any accidents. Of course, the old Chevy *was* built like a tank. It probably could have taken a few hits, or even caused some heavy damage—emotional or otherwise—without showing any battle scars. Kristie must have known something I didn't.

"Can't I just stay here?" Kristie said.

"She's afraid of your crazy driving, Mom," Scott said.

"Oh, just let her drive." Jesse said.

"You shut up, you spoiled little brat." Scott elbowed Jesse.

"All of you knock it off, or you'll be walking!"

We took a customary collective pause before anyone dared to speak again.

"Okay," Kristie said. "I'll walk home. I just need a map or something." She had decided to accept the alternative.

Jesse and Scott began laughing.

"Don't be crazy," I said. "It's forty miles, you numskull."

"That's okay, just let her walk," Jesse said.

"Maybe she can hitchhike," Scott said.

"Or, maybe Jimmy could drive me home tomorrow!" Kristie suggested.

"That's enough!" Mom shouted. "My driving is fine, so stop being so damn hysterical."

That was expected. The matter was closed. Kristie broke into doleful sobs while rain spattered the windows.

"Oh, stop your blubbering and be still," Mom said. She looked in the rear view mirror. Satisfied her hair was holding up in the weather, she tested the knot of her scarf and turned off the interior light. While Kristie whimpered, Jesse began nodding-off. Scott stared out the window, certain to drift-off too, once the car began moving. I glanced at the slab of wedding cake on the seat and decided it wouldn't make much difference to the upholstery if the plate slid around a bit. I would probably fall asleep too.

Mom finished situating herself and turned the key. The motor's rumbling blended with the rain drumming on the roof. Kristie stifled a gasp as the old gray car clunked into gear. We headed for the freeway and I settled for the ride with one eye on the wedding cake.

Driving home from Chula Vista, the night grew darker as the rain became heavier. Inside the car, with its matching gray upholstery, the interior was practically invisible except for the lighted dashboard. Outside, ahead, all we could see were the lights from other cars reflecting off the wet roads. The only sounds were of our tires rushing through the watery streets. The back seat had gone silent during the long drive. I stared at my side window and watched water droplets slipping across the glass. Drowsy from the rhythm of the windshield wipers, I nodded off.

Although our 1959 Chevy Bel Air seemed indestructible, there was something wrong with the brakes. They didn't always function the way they were supposed to. Having driven the car on frequent errands, I was well familiar with the problem. Mom had not taken the car for servicing even as the situation grew worse—*even* while she was dating a tow truck driver who might have been of some help. Someone had not been connecting the dots. Since I was not a mechanic at fourteen, and with no one around teaching me auto repair, my only immediate interest was in driving the clunker—not fixing it—which is exactly what one would expect from a teen-aged male.

We lived at the top of long hill, which made the brake problem all the more sensational. Operating the vehicle was always an urgent enterprise from the first moment upon leaving our driveway. Our street was long and steep with the other tract homes lined up the hill toward ours at the top. We would start by backing out of our driveway and pointing the gray behemoth down the hill. The battle would usually begin slowly, and then become steadily more urgent going down the hill. It took finesse and grit during the ordeal. Whenever Mom drove, there were usually near misses while running the stop sign at the bottom of the hill, explaining why Kristie stopped asking Mom for rides to school when she missed her bus.

Jimmy had given helpful advice to Mom on how to pump the brakes to build up fluid pressure in the lines. Mom had then passed the instructions on to me in a rough translation. It all really came down to just stomping on the brakes and hoping for the best. Putting the car in low gear also helped to slow the Chevy when pumping the brakes wasn't enough. However, the heavy car would most times pass through the stop sign at the bottom of the hill. After slowing down to almost a stop, the car would invariably creep onward, passing the stop sign until it was fully in the middle of the cross street. There, it would stop, assuring maximum exposure to oncoming traffic. By sheer luck, the worst we ever got were honking horns and glares from other drivers swerving to avoid us. Yet, the brakes were never fixed.

The car was still moving when I opened my eyes during the drive home from Chula Vista. The unlit road ahead was barely visible. All I could see were long streaks of rain in the headlights. Out my side windows were far off lights from cars some distance away. Mom had exited the freeway for a side road, thinking it would be safer. It looked as though we were the only car traveling on our dark road, which made it even more difficult to see. Passing the local drive-in theater, I recognized the area. We were on a curvy road running through an open tract about a half mile from our house—almost home.

Just as I was making sense of our location, the car lurched, jostling me against my door. Mom was gripping the steering wheel and turning hard, fighting for control. Despite her gritting her teeth and grunting, the Chevy was not responding and we continued barreling forward. The rear seat sprang to life as the three in the back hopped up on their knees, squealing. We hit a long stretch of water on the asphalt. Where the road turned left, the car proceeded straight ahead, hydroplaning over the puddle and skimming freely along. As Mom and I resigned ourselves to enjoying the wreck calmly, the wide-eyed conniption in the back continued with loud bawling.

Out of control, the car went into a long glide with all its weight careening into a chain link fence. The fence grabbed hold of the car by the bumper and slowed it gently, acting like a net. We made a graceful pirouette while being wrapped in chain-link, watching as it scraped against the windows. The fence finished its job with us safe in its grasp, bringing us to a quiet stop. In the silence that followed, I resisted the urge to yell, *Look! Giant spider coming!*

Our stunt left nobody physically harmed although Kristie appeared to be in a minor stupor—which seemed reasonable for her at the time. After a few moments in numb silence watching the steam rising in the headlights, a passing motorist on his way to the U-Totem noticed us and stopped. Assistance came quickly with flares and fence cutters. When our doors were finally opened and the lights came on, the first thing I noticed was the cake on the floor.

The single wedding tier had slipped its seat and landed between Mom's foot and the brake. Standing-in for the pedal, the cake had suffered a furious stomping. Even mashed, it was still recognizable as vanilla cake-stuff, slathered on the brake pedal and strewn all over the floor mats. The largest chunk showed a clean footprint from Mom's open-toed sandal. However, there wasn't enough left of the sweet souvenir to finish its journey to our freezer. It was supposed to have been kept preserved and intact with similar hopes for my brother's marriage, which had probably started-out in a back seat too.

Look where the cake ended up.

Mulvaney's Dialogue

"Are you cold, Mom?"

"*I can check your coat later on if you like, ma'am.*"

"This is nice, Bobby."

"I came here for lunch with Zach, once. I thought you might like it. The food is pretty good."

"*Can I get you anything from the bar?*"

"I'll have a gin and tonic, please—Beefeater if you've got it."

"I'll have a vodka martini—up—with an olive."

"*Right way, sir. Any preference?*"

"Smirnoff is fine, if you have it. Do you want some wine with dinner too, Mom?"

"Oh, that would be nice, Bobby."

"*Excellent, sir. I'll bring you a wine list.*"

"Okay."

"*Our special today is a seafood trio. It's scallops, shrimp, and calamari served with steamed vegetables and choice of potato or rice pilaf. It also comes with the salad bar ... I'll get your drinks while you look over the menu.*"

"Thank-you."

"Yeah, thanks ... Did he say the special comes with shrimp, Bobby?"

"Yes, he said shrimp, scallops, and calamari."

"Calamari? Ooh, I don't think I like calamari, Bobby ... Do you think I could substitute more shrimp for the calamari instead, Bobby?"

"Well, we can ask..."

"Do you think I can get a baked potato?"

"I'm pretty sure the waiter said the special comes with baked potato or rice, Mom."

"What are you having, Bobby?"

"I think I'm going to have the chicken. But you just get whatever you feel like. I'm not very hungry, so I'm just eating light."

"Oh?"

"Can I put your coat away for you, ma'am?"

"No ... I was just getting a Kleenex."

"Have you decided on lunch?"

"What did you say was on special?"

"Yes, it's a seafood medley of shrimp, scallops, and calamari."

"Ooh, I don't like calamari. I wonder if I could have extra shrimp, instead."

"Why, I'm not sure, ma'am, but I'll be glad to check with the chef."

"That would be nice. Thank-you."

"Okay ... thanks, Bobby."

"Don't worry. He'll check on it for you."

"Ma'am the chef says that's fine. The chef says he will give you extra shrimp and scallops instead of the calamari."

"Oh, I just wanted extra shrimp..."

"That's very nice of the chef, *Mom.* I'm sure it'll be fine. You *like* scallops."

"Well, that's fine, I guess..."

"I'll be happy to check with the chef again, Ma'am ... I'll mention you would prefer more shrimp."

"That's nice, Bobby."

"Mom."

"*Ma'am, I checked again and the chef is happy to give you two thirds shrimp and one third scallops with that special.*"

"Okay, well that's really good, right Mom? … I'll have the chicken."

"*Very good, sir, and that comes with—*"

"Do I get a potato with that?"

"*Oh, sorry, ma'am …uh … Yes, ma'am! Yours comes with choice of potato or rice pilaf, steamed vegetables, and salad bar.*"

"Baked potato?"

"*Yes, ma'am.*"

"Does it come with butter?"

"*Yes, ma'am.*"

"Can I have sour cream, too?"

"*Certainly, ma'am … that would be no problem at all.*"

"Chives?"

"*Of course, no problem at all.*"

"And it comes with vegetables? What kind of vegetables?"

"*I believe it is a mix of zucchini with green beans and yellow peppers.*"

"Ooh, that sounds good, doesn't it, Mom?"

"Bobby, I think I'll have the New York steak."

"I'm going to the salad bar.…"

Cy and Mindy Meechum

"USELESS is what you are! Just useless—the *two* of you!"

Tough love, some might call it—a mother shouting at her children that way. "Both of you need to get the hell out and stop coming back here!" The thing was they weren't children. They were adults.

It was not the first time Marco had heard that same tirade coming from outside his window. It always came from the same crummy little trailer in the lot behind his condominium. Cy and Mindy Meechum were trouble. Marco knew it from the first time he heard them arguing with their mother in her singlewide home. The brother and sister had parked themselves on the old lady again, making Marco's second-floor condominium a ringside seat to their disturbing frays. From his bedroom window, Marco could hear the three of them arguing day and night. They bickered constantly, and sometimes even laughed, always at barroom pitch. People in Torrance were familiar with the Meechums. As condensed as the California suburb was, everyone had at least heard of Cy and Mindy.

The younger of the two, Cy, used to pull tricks on Santa Monica Boulevard after school. He would hitch to West Hollywood to make quick cash catching johns on their way home from work.

Men would pay him for a few minutes in their cars, or rent him for a weekend in Calabasas—just once. Cy knew what to expect from the men. They were like matches that lit up and burned out quickly, leaving him with money in his pockets. He had no preferences when it came down to it. Women weren't running out and paying for it the way men did, so Cy was just following the easy money.

Mindy would not hold a steady job either. She'd work until she'd saved a little money, and then mooch for as long as she could, while actively keeping intact her reputation as a low, venomous bitch. She was difficult to look at, like a Picasso with face and body parts confused. Less than five feet tall, Mindy was a mish-mash of plaid shirts and disco pants, cowboy boots and gold chains. Her short blonde hair looked like a bad attempt at channeling James Dean. It was painful. Always angry and barking like an agitated Chihuahua, she even smiled like a snarling dog when she bared her teeth to grin. Just like a canine, too, she was protective and loyal when it came to her younger brother, Cy.

For months, their relentless cigarette smoke had flavored the air outside Marco's window as Cy and Mindy vented about their mediocre lives. Finally, Mrs. Meechum kicked them out again—for the last time. It was a welcome relief to Marco. He had long verged on paying them a visit.

Marco watched from his window the morning Cy and Mindy were leaving. Their departure was sudden and unceremonious. They had decided to pack themselves off to San Diego where nobody would know them. While Mindy sat waiting in her immaculate El Camino, their mother followed Cy to the car with a few of their bags and a couple of parting shots.

"Why can't you two learn to be more resilient? Be like other parents' grown children for chrissakes!" Dorothy Meechum said. "Get some friggin' gumption, you two!"

Before she could say another word, Mindy had stepped on the gas and the car was moving. From his condo window, Marco thought he could hear the sounds of barking coming from their car as they drove away. Their mother walked a few steps after them and then stopped.

"Cy! ... Mindy! ... Get jobs! ... Be back for Christmas!"

After the smoke had cleared, Marco continued to hear of the Meechum siblings long after he couldn't smell them anymore. Ironically, Marco was from San Diego himself, having relocated to Torrance several years prior. He had done well with investments and had no need to work again, yet there were times he had regretted leaving San Diego for his bargain retirement in Torrance.

Marco still had an attachment in San Diego, however. He had a niece named Reina, a thoughtful young woman who had grown up in San Diego, and was still living there. Marco didn't often communicate with his relatives, but he remained in touch with his niece by telephone at least a few times a year.

Within weeks of arriving in San Diego, Cy and Mindy, by sheer coincidence, became intertwined in Reina's life, although it was years before Marco ever learned of it. Reina had always been modest about her personal life, thus never mentioning Cy and Mindy to her uncle—and later coming to regret it.

"... *just another body in the refrigerator to them*," Mrs. Meechum would say later. "...*Cy and Mindy couldn't give a shit about anyone else but themselves ...*"

In San Diego, Reina had to quit school after her father died from heart failure. Her mother went to stay with a relative in Arizona while Reina insisted on remaining in San Diego. Fending for herself, she rented her first apartment in a second-class neighborhood near the factory where she had taken a job. Her building was old and in the airport flight path, so it was rundown and noisy, but it was conveniently located near to where she worked. Her job was doing piecework in a factory making men's golf clothes, ironing flat the flies of hundreds of pairs of slacks a day. The faster she flattened flies, the more money she made. It was an unremarkable living, but she was adjusting well. She had been getting used to the simplicity of life on her own when she met Cy in a bar one night.

It had never been typical of Reina to go to bars. She was considered attractive, having smooth olive skin and long dark hair, but she was uncomfortable going out alone. She had never considered herself a social person. Yet, after months in her small apartment and discovering solitude for the first time in her life, she eventually talked herself into going out instead of just being lonely at home.

Reina decided a few quiet beers or a couple of glasses of wine were okay a couple of times a week. She didn't have a television, and listening to the radio only made her feel lonelier, so to hear some noise other than the jets flying overhead, she motivated herself to go out. Going to the bar gave Reina hope, or at least something to do. She had no idea what to expect, but there was always the chance....

Reina began going to a small lounge just a short walk away from her apartment. She took to sitting quietly at the bar, yet still feeling desperate. Despite her brave efforts, she was practically unnoticed. She wouldn't let it stop her from going, though. It was still better than sitting at home alone.

"The Hut" was a small lounge mainly frequented by older gays and the occasional hustler. Reina remained a stranger, rarely speaking to anyone except to ask for a beer and avoiding becoming familiar with any of the regulars. In as ordinary a neighborhood as hers, she didn't worry about with whom she was elbowing. She just kept to herself in the dim little bar. Fortunately, given her inexperience, she was immune to feeling unnerved by lack of attention. She had become so impervious to human contact, that just a few oblivious beers were all she needed to temper her loneliness. She was usually good to just sit awhile and then go home early knowing she had at least put-in a little effort.

When Cy showed up at the bar one night, he wasn't sure what he would find either, although he was trying his best to be invisible. Fresh from boot camp, his hair was buzzed short. If the MPs caught him there, he would be hauled out of the bar and thrown into the brig. Cy immediately noticed Reina was the only true female in the darkened lounge—the only one he was certain was not a man in drag. He sat on a stool a few friendly queens over from Reina and moped in his beer until he caught her watching him. Anyone else in the small bar knew exactly what would follow. Cy waited a few minutes before approaching Reina, and then went into playing-up the away-from-home sailor, all alone, having just been ditched by his buddies.

"I've never been here before. Is this a good place to hang out?" Cy said. It was a soft approach.

"It's good enough for me." Reina said, always polite. "I'm Reina."

She held out her hand and Cy grasped it gently, and then let her take it back.

"The queen, right?" he said.

"*Yes*, very good," she said. "My mother is Spanish."

"My name is Cy. It's a king's name—as in Cyrus the *Great*."

"Really?"

"Yeah, so we're both royalty, huh? There's a *lot* of that going on around here." Cy laughed and acknowledged the nearby winks. The dynamics in the room had changed quickly since he had focused in on Reina. The two made an immediate connection, which gradually developed into an intimate evening together.

Only one night alone with Cy, and Reina was infatuated with her sailor king. Cy's fondness for Reina was unmistakable too. He was taken by the vulnerable woman whose beautiful eyes and luxurious skin had awakened something new in him. They subsequently became lost in each other for days at a time. Reina warmed to Cy as her cautious walls fell away. She found Cy to be all she had wanted. Something had come alive in her too. Thus, truths began to change for Reina.

Cy, selfishly affected by his feelings for Reina, tended to cling to her. In fact, he often alluded to Reina that he felt she belonged to him. As his possessiveness became more obvious, Reina was charmed at first. Over time, she allowed herself to be only slightly annoyed by Cy's overbearing. Even when he began asking her about her activities during the day, such as her route to and from work, and with whom she spoke with on the telephone, she still didn't allow it to bother her. She eventually came to see Cy's controlling behavior as merely familiar and tolerable. Having had no prior romantic experience as a frame of reference, Reina went along accepting Cy's behavior without resentment or feeling any loss of independence. She still had her own apartment. Even though Cy had been staying overnight most of the time, Reina remained aware that she still had her own safe haven.

Cy had immediately enlisted in the Navy upon arriving in San Diego. He lived with his sister off-and-on in a two-bedroom apartment, which Mindy had also begun sharing with a new lover, Greta. At local women's bars, Mindy and Greta had become a familiar fixture together. Greta's appearance, with her prominent misshapen nose and only one good eye was a frightful complement to Mindy's angry look. Greta usually hovered near Mindy around the pool tables, even though the two quarreled continually. Cy rarely saw the two except when home on leave. Usually, if he weren't sleeping, his primary interaction with Mindy and Greta would involve one of their arguments, in which case he would always take his sister's side. Otherwise, the navy had kept Cy preoccupied most of the time.

Mindy had right away taken a job at the telephone company upon arriving in San Diego with Cy. Working as a Directory Assistance Operator, she was earning good wages and maintaining consistent employment for the first time in her life. Even after Cy had already entered the Navy, Mindy had nagged her brother to apply for a job at the phone company too. She knew her brother well enough that she didn't think he would last in the military.

In fact, Cy did burn out quickly in the Navy. After completing basic training and then having met Reina, he decided he didn't want to see the rest of the world. He couldn't stand the idea of sea deployment and being away for months. Therefore, in order to be discharged, he blatantly lied, telling the chaplain he was gay. Cy was out of the military within weeks, following standard protocol, and was free again to roam as he pleased.

Reina had begun re-thinking her future as well. She realized her own mindless job had only limited potential. With Mindy's further prodding, both Cy and Reina applied for jobs at the phone company. Each took a placement test and waited to hear back about possible employment.

While Cy was between jobs, finances became difficult, making his situation at home awkward. Mindy and Greta were literally gnashing their teeth waiting for Cy to pay his share of the rent. Just as Cy was going to ask Reina for help, Reina, instead, turned to Cy first. A minor calamity had left Reina in an urgent bind. As she was leaving for work one morning, upon closing her apartment door, she had heard a loud crash. Returning inside, she had discovered that her kitchen ceiling and parts of her roof had collapsed, leaving an impossible mess and a gaping hole to the sky. With the season's rains approaching, Reina was forced to vacate her apartment. With Cy's coaxing, she moved in with him, finding herself fast becoming better acquainted with Mindy and Greta. Grateful to be sharing the apartment, even though it felt unfamiliar and cramped, she found an even stronger bond with Cy while adjusting to her new circumstances.

Upheavals were occurring frequently for Reina. She hadn't even had time to step back and assess where her life was going. Yet, the changes continued coming. She and Cy were both offered jobs at the telephone company. Cy was hired as an operator, like his sister, while Reina was given a better position, entering the company as a marketing representative. Cy was glad to accept his new job and was pleased with the convenience of working in the same department as his sister. Reina was ecstatic about her new prospects, but was also careful to temper her enthusiasm with modesty. It was a brilliant leap forward for her and it gave her hope for a solid future, but she had to be sensitive to the fact that she had made a better showing than Cy and Mindy. She couldn't celebrate too much. She wished her father were still alive so she could share her happiness with him.

Mindy, on the other hand, was outraged by Reina's fairing so much better than herself and her brother, taking it as sheer dumb luck that Reina had gotten a better job. She caustically voiced her opinion about it whenever she could fit it into a conversation.

"She thinks she's hot shit because she works downtown in a big office building!" Mindy would snarl to her goon, Greta, and to her brother. "Isn't that right, Cy?" She attempted to drag Cy into her campaign too, but Cy kept quiet—at least in front of Reina.

Reina was repulsed by the stupidity of Mindy's twisting her good fortune into a malicious farce. At times, she could barely contain her simmering frustration. Once, in an unguarded moment, as both Cy and Mindy were needling her about something petty, Reina lost her patience and blurted-out a fitting blast. "You guys are just a couple of trained monkeys!" she said. "Any idiot could do your jobs!" She then punctuated her remarks with an uncharacteristic sneer.

The silence that followed Reina's outburst felt as though an apocalyptic warning sign that she had made a disastrous mistake confronting the two Meechums. Although the world wasn't about to implode, she knew there were going to be consequences, but she had no idea when or how they would come.

Ironically, the telephone company would provide the very tools that Mindy would use in an attempt to exact blood from Reina. Workers at the company were all provided excellent financial programs and health benefits, which most workers appreciated for the security they provided. However, a few rare and creative employees saw the company's benefits as a resource to be tapped like a liquid asset for gain.

Mindy enlisted Cy in persuading Reina to sign up for life insurance. The two aggressively pointed out the long list of advantages. It was suggested that Reina assign Cy as her beneficiary, while Cy, in turn, would make Reina his designate. Reina agreed to the arrangement merely to avoid discord, making

Cy the sole payee of her policy, even forsaking her own family. She knew she could always change the policy later, so she signed up as agreed. With all of her good intentions and wanting to go with the flow, Reina was still too naïve to realize she was becoming her own worst enemy.

In Torrance, Marco had been enjoying peace after Cy and Mindy had moved away. He was pleased when Reina occasionally called to relate how her career was going in San Diego, and to ask how her uncle was doing. She usually spared Marco the intimate details of her life. All the while, neither Marco nor Reina realized they had both been crossing paths with the Meechums. Marco never mentioned he had often said hello to Mrs. Meechum in passing on the sidewalk. Dorothy Meechum would usually be on her way to their corner store for cigarettes while Marco might be returning home from the same with air-freshener. Likewise, Reina had never mentioned her affiliations with Cy and Mindy Meechum—even though she had been living with them for months.

One Saturday, Reina telephoned her uncle in a routine hello.

"Everything's going fine, Uncle Marco." Reina was typically bubbly over the telephone during their conversations. "I just bought a new stereo for my car!"

"That's wonderful, Rei. You still have the Mustang, right?"

"Of course I still have it, Marco. I love it!" It was her first car, a used '68 Mustang, which she had purchased just after high school, "I'm taking really good care of it, like you've told me."

"Good for you, Reina," Marco said. "I've always been jealous of that car. It's a really nice one, you know. They don't make that Shelby anymore."

"I know," Reina said. "You should see the mags I put on it."

"Mags? Ay-e-e!"

"Yes! I got the deep-dish Cragers—brushed aluminum. They look nice with the Tiger Paws, too. I already told you about the tires, right?"

"Yeah, but you need to send me some pictures. I want to put them on my refrigerator so I can dream."

They laughed. The affection between uncle and niece remained strong, no matter if it was sometimes months between conversations.

Working downtown, Reina loved the vibrant atmosphere. While the city was undergoing a robust redevelopment, so her career, too, was moving forward with stimulating challenges. Adding to her sense of accomplishment, she had also developed new friendships at work, but she was cautious to enjoy them strictly in her professional environment. Her only letdowns came usually at the end of the day, when Cy might question her if she occasionally arrived home late. Reina would feel undermined by Cy's mistrust in those instances, at times, but it became a habit for her simply to let it go. It was not in Reina's nature to give in to negativity. Rather, she preferred to move past such distractions.

Moreover, Cy had a way of instilling in Reina positive visions of their being together and of their staying together for the long haul, which served to counter any warning signs Reina might have seen in her relationship. In her optimism, Reina continued to nurture her love for Cy, finding comfort in sharing her life with him.

There were always reasons to be nervous at home, however. Mindy and Greta's relationship had begun to get ugly—even more so than usual. Over time, as familiarity gave way to contempt for one another, the two women's frequent spats became more violent. During one nasty rage, Greta actually punched a hole in the drywall and yanked the bathroom door from its hinges, even threatening Reina with a fist when she tried to intervene.

"It's like living with gargoyles!" Reina had complained to Cy.

"Don't worry, Rei," Cy had said. "Mindy knows how to handle Greta."

Ultimately, Greta did move out and a relative calm ensued in the apartment.

"It's like we've had an exorcism!" Reina had laughed. She was gleeful that Greta had gone and had made certain that Mindy knew it.

With Greta out of the way, though, Mindy had more time for conniving and asserting her will with her brother. She and Cy had been commuting to work together for months, which gave them hours of time in which to chat during their drives. Reina imagined brother and sister enjoying fuzzy familial bonding as they traveled to and from work, but anyone from Torrance would have guessed *conspiring like pirates* was more likely the case. Reina had no idea of the Meechum siblings' prior history.

Arriving home from work one evening, Cy and Mindy initiated another one of their odd discussions about insurance benefits. They suggested that all three of them increase their coverage to the maximum allowed, thus assuring a substantially larger benefit should any need arise. Mindy relished pointing out that the payout would double while the premiums would increase only slightly. Given the minor immediate impact of the change, Reina did not object. She promised to make the change to her policy, and dismissed any further discussion. The subject of insurance, to her, seemed entirely remote and unnecessary.

After a year or so, with their incomes having improved, Mindy, Cy, and Reina moved to a larger living space, a quaint cottage in the same neighborhood, with its own front yard and a picket fence. To Reina, it was a like a childhood dream house. It was a welcome move from their small apartment. Cy and Mindy added new furnishing to make the larger living area more comfortable, while Reina dug a flowerbed along the front of the house. She had always wanted to grow tulips and decided to try planting them for the first time. She bought bulbs and followed the instructions, keeping them in the freezer for a few weeks, and then planted them, looking forward to them blooming in the spring. While waiting for her tulips to come up, Reina wished Mindy would somehow find a reason to go away. She had been growing tired of the tension of having Cy's sister in the house. Yet, mindful that

Cy and his sister were very close, Reina remained patient and tolerated Mindy like a rash that wouldn't heal.

Eventually, Reina became hopeful when Mindy began seeing a young law student. It was an extraordinary lurch forward for Mindy, even though she had met her new pal, Rachel, in a bar while playing pool for cash bets. Rachel, with her college education and conservative background, was far above Mindy's social station, yet for some unfathomable reason, she enjoyed Mindy's company. Reina welcomed Mindy's new acquaintance and hoped something serious might come of it that might lead to Mindy moving out. Unfortunately, things went just the opposite way. Mindy's new refined stooge in fact osmosed into another regular vermin in their communal cottage, practically moving-in with the group. Reina was forced to white-knuckle yet another change, handling it in her usual tolerant manner.

Reina and Cy had their share of small disagreements, but by their second winter together heavy clouds of bickering were lingering over their heads. As New Year's Eve arrived, with it came one of their most bitter squalls, as if a prelude of things to come. The fighting began in a local pub on an insanely foggy night. As the couple drank with friends, a night that had began with intentions of dancing and celebration, instead turned into a loud, sloppy row. An off-hand comment was made, then another was returned, and then things escalated into a gale. The argument had not been about money or jealousy—not even about Cy's sister. However, exactly what the disagreement had been about, no one would ever recall.

When the tension had become too much for Reina and Cy to enjoy the celebration, Cy suggested they go home to ring in the New Year there, instead of disturbing the holiday crowd at the bar. Reina immediately agreed and headed for the exit while Cy followed her outside. Reina's '68 Mustang Shelby waited at the curb, barely visible in the fog. Even as protective as Reina was of her pampered car, she was not about to take the wheel after drinking and arguing. Instead, she delegated the driving to Cy.

"Here, *you* drive," she said, holding out her keys at arm's length. She could not even see her hand through the mist in the dark.

Cy took the keys from Reina's fingers with no apparent concern for his own condition or the dismal weather. He then assisted Reina into the passenger seat and closed her door. Reina watched Cy's shrouded figure bumping against the car as he walked around to the driver's side door and got in. He sat down, wiping a wet hand on his jeans.

"Fine, I'll drive then," he said, fumbling with the keys. "Just be quiet. It's foggy as hell out and I need to concentrate." Cy started the car.

"We live in the other direction, you know," Reina said. "All you need to do is turn around and go in the opposite direction and you can't miss our street."

"Don't worry. I'll get us there," Cy said. "Just be quiet and let me drive."

Cy began pulling away from the curb. Reina could only see clouds in the headlights as they began moving slowly.

Years later, in a telephone conversation with her Uncle Marco, Reina recalled the frightening details of that night. Although she could never remember what she and Cy had been arguing about, she could describe what had happened after they had come out of the bar, when they had begun driving in the thick fog.

"We couldn't see any more than two feet in front of the car," Reina said, as her uncle listened. "I remember wondering how Cy could even see where he was driving," she said. "He even had to open his door and look down at the white line in the street. It was the only way he could tell where we were going … I still can't believe it."

"What a fool, eh? How could he do that?" Marco said. "What did you do?"

"Well, listen. It get's worse …"

Reina admitted that as they drove, between the dense clouds and the darkness, and her having drunk too much, she was too confused to keep her bearings, even forgetting that Cy was going in the wrong direction.

"I didn't even realize he was still going west. I had told him to turn around. We lived east!"

Cy drove all the way to the end of the street, where an enclave of exclusive condominiums sat on the edge of a canyon, high above Mission Valley. There, the road turned sharply to the left, following the rim of a wide-open canyon. The view was spectacular, but the drop from the edge was hundreds of feet into a ravine. They were heading straight toward the edge in the fog.

Reina remembered how she raised her head to look, just as they reached the end of the street. Cy had failed to turn left and was continuing straight into a wooden barricade.

"I looked up and saw this big yellow sign with red reflectors all sparkling in the headlights. I had no idea what I was doing there. I had never been to that end of the street, so I was confused. I thought I was dreaming."

She recalled seeing a small DEAD END sign on a fence, as they kept on moving forward. She watched in horror out her side window as the car continued past the sign and crashed through the barrier. What happened next was a blur.

"I remember the car turning over because I put my hands up to try and stop my head from hitting the ceiling," Reina said. "I was trying to brace myself. I remember touching the fabric on the ceiling, you know?"

"My God…" Marco said. "How *scary*."

"I remember coming up and out of my seat when the car was flipping-over. They said it must have turned over three or four times. It was like being on the rock-o-plane ride at the carnival, Uncle Marco." Reina was more excited, the more she spoke. "The car actually went end-over-end, Marco. All four wheels came off! Can you believe that?"

"That's crazy, Reina."

"I blacked out and somehow survived it. I wasn't even wearing a seatbelt."

"Incredible."

"They said being drunk probably saved me."

"Yeah, you were probably flopping around like a rag doll."

They shared a brief laugh, as Reina continued describing what she had been keeping bottled-up for so many years.

An Emergency Rescue Team found Reina in her car at the bottom of the canyon. Rappelling down the ravine on ropes, they discovered the car resting on its left side with Reina slumped against the driver's side door, unconscious. It had taken nearly an hour to gurney her up from the bottom. In the hospital, a police officer stood by as doctors and nurses attended to Reina and stitched up a small cut over her eyebrow. They marveled at how she had come out of the accident without any broken bones. As she faded in and out of consciousness, the officer remained near Reina's side in the emergency room, pestering her for a blood sample, saying it was needed for an accident report. In her confusion, Reina refused the officer's requests, brushing him away several times, aggravated by his intrusiveness.

"Where is Cy? How is Cy?" Reina had worried the doctors by asking the same questions repeatedly. As a precaution, she was kept several hours, and then released to go home around noon. She couldn't recall who had driven her home.

At home, Cy had shown Reina a few minor cuts on his lower back. He had not been seriously hurt, but he explained how he had been scratched by broken window glass while climbing out of the wrecked car and then had scaled the canyon to get help. He was otherwise not even bruised. Reina was impressed by Cy's heroics and relieved he had come away unhurt. What she had not realized then was that things were worse than they had seemed, even though there hadn't been any major injuries.

After several days off from work, Reina was recovering well from her aches and bruises. The initial trauma of the accident had subsided. Then, all at once, problems began surfacing. Reina received a summons from the court about her having refused a blood alcohol test after the accident. The State wanted to revoke her license. She was also being cited for drunk driving, when she had not even been driving the vehicle. In addition, she was being billed by the city for replacing the destroyed barrier, road signs, and fencing. On top of everything else, Reina was being ordered to remove her wrecked car from the bottom of the canyon. It was a huge mistake and it was all in Reina's name. The new developments threw Reina for another loop.

Reina was fully aware that she had not been driving and she could prove it. Surely, Cy must have told the police he had been driving during the accident. If there was a mistake, all he needed to do was go to court and tell them. The charges against Reina would then be dropped and that would be the end of it. After all, it was too late to charge Cy with any crime at that point.

After her initial panic and then realizing Cy could clear up the entire mess, Reina discussed matters with him, expecting him to assure her all would be straightened out.

"Yeah, don't worry about it, Rei," Cy said. "My sister says they'll reduce the charges and it won't cost that much."

Hearing Cy's response, Reina's mind took a jag. She didn't understand Cy's meaning, exactly. She had not heard what she had expected to hear and things were not clicking.

"What do you mean *reduce the charges?*" Reina was a little dazed as she spoke.

"Don't worry. We'll work it out," Cy said. He brushed off Reina's concerns.

Cy's suggestion still would not sink in. Reina's confused psyche stopped-cold, leaving her stuck. She simply could not reconcile the resistance she was getting from Cy. It was unfathomable that Cy would not take immediate responsibility for the accident. How could he not want to cooperate? Nevertheless, Cy continued to defer discussion, saying his sister's lawyer friend was looking into it.

Reina fairly shut down for a couple of days, her mind going in circles, thinking about her situation. Reducing the charges was not going to be acceptable. She wanted everything dismissed and off her record. The repercussions were far too great for her to take the blame. Her auto insurance costs alone would sky rocket. It was all too much for her to take after the accident.

She endured a succession of sleepless nights, still aching from her injuries, until one morning a new kind of painful awareness came over her all at once, in a wave of regret. It was suddenly clear to Reina she was dealing with a front, united against her, in Cy and Mindy. Their interests lay only in the outcome for Cy regardless of the ramifications for Reina. She began to discover a resentment she hadn't experienced before, yet at the same time, she felt a need to stay above the fray. She knew she was smarter than the two half-wits she was dealing with, but her emotions were mixed, having suddenly wised-up. Determined to rise to the challenge, she convinced herself she could persuade the brother and sister to come to their senses.

Reina's first focus became getting back to her job. Since the accident, she had been receiving well wishes and cards from her associates at work whose kindnesses had raised her spirits. Despite a pouring rain on the day she returned downtown, Reina felt relieved to be back in her office among friends, away from the unsettled atmosphere at home. She felt more clear-headed and buoyant as she enjoyed a full day's work.

Riding home on the bus in the rain, Reina decided to have another talk with Cy, and possibly Mindy too, about how to deal with matters of the accident. A court appearance was nearing and Cy's cooperation would be crucial. Although work was going well, she still needed to deal with the pressing home matters.

Stepping off the bus Reina walked the short distance home, glad that the rain had let up after coming down hard all day. As she reached the cottage and entered the gate, the first thing Reina noticed was her flowerbed of tulips. She had been fascinated by how quickly they had come up in the period after the accident, the stalks growing tall in only a short time. That morning as she was leaving for work, the flowers appeared almost ready to open. Now, she was dying to see their vibrant colors. As she approached the flowerbed with her dozen tulip plants lined up along the cottage wall, what she found shocked her. Bright petals of yellow and pink lay muddy and strewn about the soil beneath empty stalks. Her flowers had been pulverized by rainwater gushing down from the roof—*on their very first day of bloom*. The stalks had been left standing naked along the mud-spattered wall. Her beautiful flowers had been ruined—another disaster she had not seen coming—*on her first day back at work*. For a minute, Reina was unable to move. She stood staring at her tulips in disbelief, feeling a pending onslaught of grief waiting to take hold. She had thought she had outgrown such vulnerability after her father had died.

Her mind then affected a kind of damage control. Something clicked, shielding Reina from her anguish. Before she could become caught up in useless self-pity, she came to grips with her emotions just in time to fend off a storm of tears. She realized she had to face Cy and Mindy inside their cottage. She knew she wouldn't get any sympathy from them. In fact, she might even be ridiculed by the Meechum duo. She went to the front door and let herself in, pushing aside thoughts of her tulips.

Entering the cottage, Reina was surprised to find Cy and Mindy behaving jovially and oddly cordial toward her.

"Sorry about your tulips, Rei," Cy said. He smiled, meekly.

"Yeah, it's too bad they all got smashed to smithereens, huh?" Mindy sniggered as Reina took note of her satisfied grin.

There was take-out food waiting, which Mindy had bought, and Cy had opened a bottle of wine. Reina decided to put off any serious discussions, feeling drained and confused in just the few minutes since she had come home.

During dinner, Cy and Mindy announced plans to visit their mother in Torrance. They were leaving the next evening and would likely be returning very late. Not wanting Reina to feel lonely, Cy and Mindy had arranged for a friend to keep Reina company while they were away. One of Cy's favorite co-workers, Clarice, had suggested she take Reina to the movies. Reina was flattered by the idea, and accepted the offer. Tired after a full day, and feeling slightly dizzy, Reina went to bed early.

The next evening, Clarice arrived just in time to greet Cy and Mindy as they were leaving. After exchanging introductions and then quick goodbyes, Cy and Mindy departed, and Reina and Clarice headed out for the evening too. Clarice had already selected a movie for her and Reina to see, although without consulting Reina. The movie she had chosen was *Endless Love*, starring Brooke Shields. Reina went along with the plans, not wanting to be rude, but regretted not having discussed it. As she watched the depressing film, she found herself becoming agitated. It was the most unmercifully gut-wrenching movie she had ever seen. The longer it went on, the more unnerved she became. Already vulnerable with her own personal crises, by the time the movie ended, Reina was left feeling even more drained. She found herself wanting to be near Cy and wishing he had not gone to Torrance with his sister. As Reina and Clarice exited the theater, Reina noticed Clarice was unaffected by the movie, having come away with nothing to say. Reina, feeling uncomfortable, feigned a headache and asked Clarice to take her home. Clarice obliged and abruptly dropped Reina curbside at the cottage with a brief goodbye. The arranged rendezvous had been a minor disaster and Reina was glad to be home, even if it meant being alone for the rest of the evening.

Opening the door, Reina noticed right away a change inside the cottage. Things were missing. It wasn't that Cy and Mindy weren't in the living room watching television as usual. It was that the television set itself was actually gone! Also gone were the audio system, books, and numerous other personal effects. As Reina moved through the apartment, she began to feel faint. Her heart pounded as she opened closets and looked in half-empty drawers. Her hands were trembling and her ears began ringing as she suddenly realized what a nightmare her life had become. Cy—*that coward*—and his despicable sister had heartlessly deserted her, leaving only their old furniture. Nearly every trace of the them had disappeared. They had packed up and gone without a single civilized word. Even worse, they had set-up Reina with their conniving friend to go and see that sickening movie while they cleared out the cottage. *Clarice had been in on it.* Reina's skin crawled realizing her companion for the evening had known all along what she would find when she came home.

After going through the entire cottage and becoming thoroughly depressed, Reina sank to the floor and sat. What pained and confused her most was that all traces of Cy were gone—*he was gone.* She sifted through a pile of old photographs she found in a corner. All of the photos had only images of her. Angry and hurt, she berated herself for having been so blind—*I'm such a sap!* Once again, she shifted into survival mode, her self-preservation autopilot kicking-in as she sat alone in the nearly empty cottage, thinking.

Digging through a box of old Christmas cards, Reina discovered an envelope with a return address for Dorothy Meechum. Reading the envelope with her hands still shaking, she was surprised to see the address was on the same street as her Uncle Marco's condo in Torrance. In fact, the number was very close. *Dorothy Meechum—Cy and Mindy's mother.* Reina knew then where to look for her former housemates. She couldn't hold back a laugh as she decided to go and visit her uncle—by way of his neighbor. She would go that night.

Reina traveled fast on the freeway in a rented car, at first listening to music and then turning it off. All the radio stations between Tijuana and Los Angeles were repeatedly playing the same nauseating theme, "Endless Love." After switching off the radio, Reina used the driving time to reflect on recent events and to try to calm herself, but by the time she reached Torrance, she was still anxious to stop by the Meechum residence. She wanted to let Cy and Mindy know that she knew where to find them and that she was not as helpless as they may have thought.

Driving on her uncle's street, Reina found the address and the small trailer court next to Marco's condominiums. She turned onto a narrow lane lined with mobile homes on either side. She was anticipating a confrontation and was feeling nervous. Half way down, she found the Meechum mailbox on a post in front of a faded pink trailer. She stopped and glanced over at the flimsy diggings. Not wanting to lose her nerve, she exited the car, walked up to the stoop, and knocked on the door. Mrs. Meechum answered quickly, surprising Reina. Cy and Mindy were not there. The exchange between Reina and Dorothy Meechum was brief.

"They were probably trying to kill you, dear!" Mrs. Meechum said. She laughed as she spoke with Reina. "I'm sure you were just another body in the refrigerator to them…"

Dorothy Meechum practically gloated in Reina's face. It was a quick but revealing meeting, and yet another blow to Reina's sensibilities. Mrs. Meechum only reinforced the harsh reality, even shouting after Reina as she was leaving the trailer park.

"Those two couldn't give a shit about anyone except themselves!" The words echoed as Reina drove away.

The Torrance encounter had been the final rude surprise. Reina had discovered even more than she had wanted to know, questions and answers that would take a long time to settle in her mind. She couldn't accept the idea she may have been set up for her insurance money. The idea of people she knew trying to kill her simply did not gel. In fact, it was a long time before she was able to speak about it—having been unable to grasp things fully, until several years had passed.

"I had pretty much put it all out of my mind, Uncle Marco." Reina continued on the telephone with her uncle. "I think I was just so blown away I just couldn't believe what Mrs. Meechum had said."

The pieces of the past were all finally falling into place while speaking about it a decade later.

"You had had enough," Marco said. "You and me, we just don't know people like that. They're bad. … You just didn't see it then."

"I was pretty gullible." Reina said.

Marco heard a smile in Reina's voice on the phone and he chuckled. "You know, all this time, I never knew you even knew the Meechums," he said. "I wish I had known."

"I had thought I was going to surprise you one day with some good news about me and Cy," Reina said.

Recalling events just then, Reina realized how blind she had been. It had begun to seem almost comical.

"It's so strange," Marco said. "When I spoke with Mrs. Meechum a couple of days after the service, she told me those two were on their way home from seeing her when—when it happened."

"Really? They were actually visiting her?"

"Yeah, but it must not have gone very well," Marco said. "From the way Dorothy was talking, she didn't seem very upset … about them dying. I probably shouldn't be saying anything about that, eh?"

"Don't worry, Marco." Reina said. She had an urge to laugh. "Gosh, I really hadn't even thought about them for years. You know, the last time I saw Cy was over five years ago," she said. "I took one of my girlfriends to a little bar in my old neighborhood. We just went for laughs. I wanted to see if it was the same."

"Oh, that's always fun, eh?" Marco laughed again.

"Well, I couldn't believe my eyes, Marco—I saw *Cy* in there!"

"You did?"

"Yes! And he was a *mess*. I swear. He looked like he was trying to pick up old men."

"You're kidding me!"

"No. It was pathetic. He was wearing old walk shorts from the '70s—and he was fat!" Reina was enjoying herself, laughing.

"Reina, that's not nice," Marco scolded.

"I know. I shouldn't laugh. We left the bar before he saw me, but you should have seen him. It was so … weird … but yeah, you're right. I shouldn't laugh." She continued laughing anyway until Marco spoke again.

"They said it was a pretty nasty accident." Marco said.

Reina had only heard sketchy details. "Wasn't there a truck involved or something?" she said.

"Yeah, but you probably don't want to know—"

"I heard there was a load of produce or something."

"No. It was one of those big lumber trucks." Marco said. "They said some maniac in a speeding car almost side-swiped it—it was crazy."

"So? What happened?"

"They said the truck—it was one of those huge eighteen-wheelers—it tried to swerve to get out of the way. The speeding car just came out of nowhere and almost hit it. When the truck tried to move over fast, its load fell off ... the chains must've broke."

"Chains? What chains?" Reina said.

"The chains that were holding the logs. All these huge trees fell off and smashed Cy and Mindy's car. It was a lumber carrier—for crying out loud—and these gigantic logs fell off it and right on top of their car."

"*Oh, my god.*"

"They never knew what hit 'em ..."

"*Wow.*"

"Can you imagine?"

Marco waited for Reina's reaction.

"Smashed like *cockroaches*—" Reina began to laugh.

"*Reina ...*"

"—to smithereens." Reina laughed even harder.

Marco didn't say anything for a moment, but Reina could hear him laughing on the other end of the telephone too.

Reina hadn't lingered long with Mrs. Meechum the night she had driven to Torrance. After hearing that Cy and Mindy were still in San Diego and that they were setting up a new apartment, Reina had felt sick with anger. She was just another body in the refrigerator to them. She had turned around and driven straight back home to San Diego that night. She hadn't even stopped to see her uncle. Instead, she went home, packed up, and moved out.

Living with a friend for a while, Reina pulled herself together and bounced back, which didn't take very long. She changed her insurance policy at work, and even took care of the nasty lingering business from the accident. After that, Reina completely shut out of her mind anything to do with the Meechums and moved on with her life.

It felt good to be talking about her difficult past with her uncle, after so much time. She was finally sorting out some of the forgotten details.

"It's strange, the things that come to mind now," Reina said. "I remember when I went back to work—it was a couple of weeks after the car accident—or, maybe I should say, *when Cy drove me off the cliff. …*" She paused. "You know, he probably *did* do that. He probably wasn't even *in* the car, now that I think of it. I'll bet he just pushed the car over the cliff with me in it."

Marco listened without responding.

"Anyway," Reina said, "my boss put flowers on everyone's desks in the office. Each person got one flower and a little card …"

"That was nice …"

"… and I just now realized something else: I think my boss did it just for me."

Marco listened.

"My boss must have put all those flowers on everyone's desks and it was probably all just for my benefit."

"Wow. You think so?"

"Yeah, I'm sure of it, now. Each little card had one word printed on it," Reina said. "I don't remember what the other peoples' cards said, but mine …"

Reina explained how she had found a single white rose on her desk with a plain white card beside it. On the card, there was one simple word printed neatly in the middle:

"Resilient."

Marco lost his breath upon hearing the word. He recalled how Mrs. Meechum had used the same word with Cy and Mindy when she had berated them for not being more like other parent's children.

"That's your word, Reina," Marco said. "Resilient—that's you. You're a resilient person, Reina, and your father would be proud of you."

"Oh, Uncle Marco, thank you," Reina said.

Marco began to chuckle.

"Now, what?" Reina said.

"Dogs barking," he said. He recalled, just then, the sounds he had thought he had heard coming from Mindy's car when she and her brother were driving away from their mother's house, years prior.

"What dogs?" Reina responded.

"Oh, nothing," Marco said. "It's not important." He changed the subject. "Hey, how did it go with your car insurance? Whatever happened after all that crap? Did you get stuck with all that mess?"

"Yeah, pretty much," she said. "My rates were really high for a long time, but they went back down a couple of years ago. There's nothing on my record anymore, but *damn* it sure cost me a lot."

"I'll bet."

"Cy never showed up for the DMV hearing," Reina said, "so they let me keep my license. I didn't even have to pay for the property damage, either. I still got screwed, though. I think my old car is still at the bottom of that canyon."

"That's funny!" Marco burst out laughing on the phone. "I mean—not *funny*. I mean the car—if it's still there—maybe we can go and get it. We could fix it up!"

Reina began laughing too.

"You're such a dreamer, Marco."

"Yeah, I know." Marco said. He was gazing out his window at the lot next door with the pink trailer. "Yeah, it's just too bad, though," he said. He could see Mrs. Meechum in the distance, coming down the street with her grocery bags.

"What do you mean?" Reina said. "What's too bad?"

"Well, you know, it cost you so much. It's just doesn't seem fair ..."

"Yeah," Reina said. "Well ... I don't know. ... Think about what happened to Cy and Mindy."

Pine Tree Privy

I'M A PINE TREE. Yes, that's what I said. I'm that pine you never notice at the intersection—the one with the sagging branches, with the long dusty needles. Pay attention. It's the house on the northwest corner. You drive past me all the time. I look like one of those pines you would see growing up on the bluffs overlooking the ocean, up by the golf course. You know, those dramatic pines that lean into the wind, hundreds of feet above the surf, hanging over the sides of the cliffs. I can only imagine what it must be like for them. I look like one of those pines. Although, instead of posing above the beach, I'm stuck here in front of this tract house where no one pays any attention to me. What a bore. Well, it's not always boring. We *do* whisper, we pines. I can tell you a few things.

Where the streets intersect here, it has become rather busy. Can you believe E Street now has four lanes? Second Avenue still has only two, but it used to be quiet around here. Now, there are stoplights and traffic. *Stoplights*—one on each corner. This *used* to be a quiet neighborhood.

Did you hear about the van that rolled down the hill? A van actually rolled down the street, downhill. Well, it was pushed. People had just begun eating dinner when it happened. A fast moving car smacked into the side of the van after the car ran the light. I saw some of it, but only heard most of it because I can't see past the other side of the intersection. They said the van driver was okay. *There are pine trees at the bottom of the hill, you know.* It was funny—the way it happened. The sides of the van were flat, so it sounded like a giant toolbox being kicked down the hill as it went rolling over. You could count each turn as it smacked the pavement, one side at a time, going down the hill with each turn making a loud clunk. I'm sure the pine trees at the golf course never hear anything like that, but I sure did.

I've been living at this corner for almost twenty-three years. I've been right here and seen it all, yet no one even notices me. I was once a more lavish pine. I started out nice and symmetrical, almost like a good Christmas tree. I was tall and straight. I could hold my branches out sideways the way people hold out their arms when they're checking for rain. Unfortunately, they had to trim me after about a dozen years. I was getting too close to the telephone wires. They just sawed off my top half and that was that. Now, I'm flat and bushy and my branches hang down to the ground. I'm okay, though. I'm not complaining. It's just that nobody ever notices me. I'm just a weird looking pine tree, sitting a few feet away from the stoplight at the corner.

I'm being upstaged by this stoplight. I might as well be invisible being so close to that bright yellow pole on the sidewalk. All that contraption does is stand there and make clicking noises while its lights change colors. I suppose the signals are useful for the children crossing the intersection. They need to get across safely on their way to school. It's funny when one of the lights burns out, though. People get so confused.

Our elderly neighbor fell and died here, near the base of the pole. He was a nice old man. He used to trim both sides of the hedge between his house next door and this one. He liked to walk in the mornings. It had something to do with a heart attack. He couldn't get to his pills. He managed to pull the little bottle out of his pocket, but then he dropped it. It rolled right underneath here, under my branches. It's hard to reach in here if you're having a heart attack, I suppose. My pine needles tend to poke you in the face as you lean in. That never stopped the young boy who lived here in the house, though. He was watching from the window on that morning when they found the old man's pills beneath one of my boughs. The boy had secret things hiding under my branches and he was afraid they would find them. He felt sad for the old man too.

The boy liked to hide under my branches. I was his fort when he didn't have anyone to play with. For a pine tree, I make a decent hideout. In fact, with my low branches, I am the perfect place for hiding things and for spying on people. He was the only boy who knew how to push aside my branches and slip underneath to sit by my trunk. It's like being inside a tent. I always have plenty of pine needles on the ground—very comfortable for sitting. With all the sap stains the kid got on his hands and clothes, I can only imagine the kind of trouble the boy must have gotten into with his mother.

The boy would giggle and hold his breath as he peeked out at the people going by on the sidewalk—with nobody knowing he was watching. No one heard him, except me, but he talked and laughed quietly to himself all the time. The boy had secret valuables he liked to hide in my little fortress too. He'd pull things out of his pockets and hang them on my trunk, on the stubs where branches had broken off. On one little nub, he hung an old rabbit's foot on a key chain. He also put a solid gold ring on one of the higher branches. He wanted to be sure it was well hidden. It looked like an old wedding band. To the boy, the ring was magical. He imagined it once belonged to a leprechaun who might be missing it. It was the boy's most valued secret treasure, yet he wished a little man in a green suit would come looking for it. Well, who wouldn't want to meet a leprechaun? He was an imaginative kid. When school began, he didn't come hiding here as often.

You might have noticed me on the night there was a fire here at the house. It was around Christmastime. The boy was going to sing with the school choir that evening. It was one of those holiday shows for the parents and families. The boy had a special part in the production where he was going to introduce an old-fashioned Christmas song the choir was to sing. He had been practicing his lines in private, underneath my branches. On the evening of the show, while the boy was eating dinner with his brothers and sisters, black smoke began billowing from the garage. It was coming from the clothes dryer that was operating with the boy's choir robe inside. The machine had overheated and caught fire! There was an awful lot of excitement with sirens blaring and the fire department coming in a big red truck—which they parked right next to me. Did you happen to notice me then?

They managed to put out the fire in the dryer before it could spread, but the boy's white robe and its big red bow were scorched brown—completely unwearable! One of the choir parents driving past was startled to see all the commotion—but she probably didn't notice me next to the fire truck, either. As soon as she reached the school, someone called to inquire about the boy. They assured the boy's mother they had another robe waiting for him to wear. By the time the boy arrived at the school that evening—only minutes before the performance—all were talking about the fire. He was the center of attention backstage, before the show.

A short time later, with the performance going well, the boy slipped away from the choir, unnoticed. When it was time for the special song, he came quietly from the rear of the darkened auditorium, catching the audience by surprise—and dressed like an old woman! Imagine that. *Who is this old loon, coming in?* No one in the house recognized the boy. He wore an oversized shawl covering his head and a loose skirt over his rolled-up trousers. Fussing and hobbling, he came up the aisle like a feisty old crone, muttering in a shaky voice like an angry old granny. The audience was convinced he was someone's actual grandma who had come while in temporary leave of her senses. They all turned in their seats to gawk.

"Hold on just a *durned* minute!" the youngster hollered as he made an old ham of himself all the way up the aisle. He even poked a few chairs with his wooden cane as he went. Acting bothered, the boy wobbled past the main stage and the choir, and stepped up onto a special stage set off to one side. A small, lighted Christmas tree stood waiting on the raised platform. As colors glowed between pine needles behind him, the granny-boy took his presence under a white spotlight. The silent audience prepared to listen.

"How's about a good *old-fashioned* song of Christmas!" the boy squawked loudly. He had gained the audience's full attention. Then he launched into a spirited speaking-to, directed toward the choir, as the audience sat in witness, listening reverently. In a stern plea for tradition, the excited granny regaled the chorus, ranting about the olden times when they had sung with joined hands and had danced 'round the Christmas tree. He went on about turkeys turning on the spit and about snow coming down two-feet-thick. For added effect, the boy began waving his old-lady cane in the air—several times nearly striking the spotlight hanging over his head! Each time he barely missed, the audience gasped and sniggered. He kept them holding their breath throughout his turn in the spotlight.

When the boy had finished his cantankerous speech, he then stepped down off the side stage, walked back onto main, and took his place on the risers with the rest of the chorus. The audience applauded warmly as the granny stood and grinned. Then, all-at-once he pulled off the shawl to reveal his short blonde hair, and became just the little boy in the chorus, again. The audience gasped and burst into laughter as the boy blinked and smiled. There were catcalls and cheers as he laughed and bowed, and his choir director stood by beaming. His timing had been flawless.

When the laughter and buzz had settled down, the chorus did just as the old lady had prescribed. They stomped their feet and clapped their hands, and sang a rousing version of the old time favorite, "'Round and 'Round the Christmas Tree." The audience clapped and stomped along, happily excusing the old lady for her precocious interruption.

The next day, the boy came and sat under my branches again. He talked quietly to himself about how famous he had been at school—although it only lasted a few days.

The boy eventually grew up and moved away. They moved on.

Maybe you've seen him around. Maybe he became even *more* famous.

I'm still here. I'm still just a dusty old pine tree with secrets to tell. You've probably driven by me a thousand times—I'm still here at the intersection. I'm not going anywhere. Maybe you'll notice me the next time. Honk, if you want.

Honk if you're that little boy. I've still got your ring!

Chance and Keanan, Adagio for Windowpane and Gazebo

"Here, drink this." Chance said. He gave Keanan a tall, plastic *Star Wars* cup full of liquid and ice. The cup was sweating and dripping on Keanan as he sat in Chance's car.

"Crap! Now my *balls* are wet!" Keanan laughed and held it away so it could drip onto the floor mat.

"Just drink it," Chance said, "and don't spill it in my car."

Several drops had already slid down the vinyl seat, between Keanan's legs, wetting his crotch. He took a taste from the straw. There were only three brown soda choices at the Circle-K.

"Big deal, 'Doctor *looks-like-I-peed-my-shorts* Pepper,'" he said, taking another sip. He swiped at more drips on his shirt.

Chance grinned. "How is it?"

"I don't know," Keanan said. "It's just soda—"

Keanan wasn't sure how to read the smirk on Chance's face. He decided to ignore it, a learned habit with his friend. Still, he worried he could be in for a surprise.

Chance drove them to La Jolla Cove in his cheap new sedan while Keanan drank his soda and admired the scenery. He rolled down his window as they braked down the steep hill to the cove. The cobblestone road was unique to the village and the car vibrated as it went over the uneven surface. It was a good night to kill time by the ocean—quiet and not jammed with tourists—just another odd work night not entirely wasted. They needed an escape from their hot apartment. Keanan had been working all day at his office job. Chance had the night off from his security post at the art museum, a hundred yards from the cove.

As they drove, Keanan looked toward the bluffs for the wooden gazebo.

"There it is," he said.

"What?"

"Nothing. Just the gazebo."

It stood exactly where it always was, overlooking the ocean near the edge of the bluffs.

"You and the gazebo," Chance said. He could feel Keanan's strange obsession with the kiosk.

The sight of the gazebo always made Keanan feel lonely for it. With its dark green paint, the little wooden booth appeared cold and utilitarian like an old tool shed. It seemed to begrudge its position. Beyond the gazebo, far more stimulating was the expansive ocean itself, broadcasting the entire curve of the horizon. Even on the brightest spring days, the gazebo sat forgotten and cheerless, juxtaposed against the sea.

"It's weird to see this place so quiet." Chance steered the curve at the bottom of the hill. "When I come to work in the afternoon, it's always crawling with tourists, you know?"

Where the road came closest to the cove, the sidewalk skirting the cliffs was deserted. Keenan's eyes followed the long handrail next to the cliff's edge. The only barrier before a dangerous drop, it was constructed of metal pipes linked together like tinker toys. At the bottom of the rocky bluffs is a slender crescent of sand. A small portion of the sea pushes and shoves its way into the scenic inlet. There are dangerous small caves surrounding the cove too, but the experienced locals avoid any exhilarating temptation to explore them.

People come to watch the sea lions on the rocks while wet-suited surfers paddle in from the offshore waves. The elements always threaten, but they've only taken a few lives in a long history of mostly drowning near misses. Recent years have passed without a fatality.

Keanan noticed the gazebo was empty. "Don't you think it's weird, there's never anyone in the gazebo?"

"Yeah, it's like we're practically the only ones using it," Chance said. *So what?* he thought.

Keanan imagined the gazebo as feeling intimidated in the spectacular setting. More than that, he believed the gazebo possessed a consciousness as though it were a secret spiritual repository of local lore.

"Did you drink some?" Chance asked.

"Yes, it's fine … *why?*" Keanan was suspicious again. "Did you put something in it?"

Chance scanned the large selection of available parking. With the area so quiet, he could pull over almost anywhere.

"It's only a little mushroom extract," Chance said. He hoped Keanan would buy it, but he knew he probably wouldn't. He chuckled to himself, anticipating his friend's reaction.

"Are you kidding me?" Keanan said. "It's a *work* night for me! I've got to be at work in the morning!"

The gazebo remained restrained in the distance, quietly listening, unnoticed.

"Seriously, Chance, what is this?" Keanan pulled the top off his plastic cup and looked inside at the soda and ice.

"Don't worry—"

"What's this?" Keanan fished out a small object from his drink, examining a flat square on his fingertip. It appeared to be a piece of thick paper or cardboard with colored art imprinted on it, as though cut out from a comic book cover. There were dot patterns in the print, like the shading in a Warhol lithograph.

"Well, you said you might want to try it," Chance said.

Keanan then realized what Chance had put in his drink,

which made the situation even worse. Keanan had never intended to try windowpane—not acid. It had always been entirely out of the question and in a whole other league for a different breed. It was partially his own fault, he realized, however. He should have known Chance would take such liberty. Even so, it was pointless to challenge the scruples of someone who lacked any. Keanan resolved not to give in to anger, instead plunging straight into denial and hoping to avert disaster. He already knew there was no such thing as mushroom extract. He was unwittingly heading into Alice's rabbit hole and he knew it, having been thrown down it and not having jumped to the next realm of pharmaceutical exploration voluntarily. Maybe it wouldn't do anything at all.

They were supposed to just go and sit in the gazebo awhile. There was no particular reason other than it was a better way to pass the time than sitting in their stuffy apartment watching television all night. Now that Chance had conspired to make their excursion more interesting, Keanan tried not to think about it although inside he was secretly curious, seduced by his fascination with a highly precarious unknown.

Chance and Keanan could have spent a late night out shooting pool and dealing with a next-day hangover. Instead, they went to the cove just as they had several other times. Smoky bars were not on the agenda this time. Chance's experiment required breathing room. The gazebo, their usual hangout, seemed a suitable spot for drinking doctored soda. Since it lacked romantic charm and didn't attract much attention, any odd behaviors would likely go unnoticed. Keanan zipped his jacket as they neared the park. Their little clubhouse wasn't designed as a shelter from the wind.

The gist of the gazebo, to Keanan, was in its embedded secrets—the confessions whispered by strangers within its walls, and the knife-carved epitaphs worked into its wood. Keanan already believed the gazebo listened. He imagined a day when giddy scientists, using some future technology, would be able to unlock its legends. Only then would it begin talking. It would finally spill it and be noticed. Keanan wondered how the gazebo might judge. He wondered if his friend Chance and he would become indelible in its memory.

Adjacent to the cove and surrounding the gazebo was well-manicured park. Although usually too noisy to enjoy during the day, it was quiet when Chance and Keanan pulled up. The park was empty and it appeared they would have it all to themselves. As done before, they would sit in the gazebo and listen to waves hashing it out on the rocks below the bluffs. Chance parked his car and the two friends got out, taking in the salt air.

To reach the gazebo required a walk across a long stretch of trim lawn spanning the park, leaving behind the local boutiques and cafes. About mid-way across the green, the sounds from the town faded. For several yards there was near silence until they could hear the ocean as they neared the gazebo.

"Are you feeling anything, Kean?" Chance was gauging his experiment.

"I'm fine." In truth, Keanan was not exactly sure how he was. They continued walking across the grass.

The gazebo was always dark. Even during the day, the light remained dim under its roof and within its short walls. At night, the shadows were confusing, but Chance and Keanan were well familiar with the spot. Beyond the structure, north, the view was all ocean. The Pacific was a magnificent panorama during the day, but by night, it was visible only as random whitecaps illuminated by whatever little light could reach its swells from shore. Facing south, Chance and Keanan's view was of the park they had just crossed. Looking back, the grass appeared black in the dark except for a few stretches lit by the floodlights aiming in from the street. Any noises from the town didn't reach the gazebo.

They took their places sitting on the half walls of the kiosk and fixed their gazes over the lawn. Like a silent movie, they watched the few runners and dog walkers pass on the distant street, unheard beyond the floodlights.

"I love looking back from here," Keanan said.

"Yeah, I know what you mean." Chance's face was hidden in the gazebo's shadows. "What a trip, huh?"

"Yeah, it's freakin' *brilliant* is what it is!" Keanan said.

Chance laughed, caught off guard by Keanan's sudden gush.

The two were invisible in the gazebo from the street, obscured by the lit-up lawn in front of them. It was an impish thrill to be lurking in the shadows, the ocean pounding the cliffs behind them.

Keanan zipped his jacket a little higher. "Do you know what *La Jolla* means?" He glanced toward Chance in the shadows. "It means, *the jewel*, in Spanish." He was offering a fascinating bit of trivia.

"No shit, Sherlock. I grew up here, brah,'" Chance knew more about the area than Keanan.

With the wind at their backs, in their light jackets, they sat and watched the scenery.

"It looks like a big theater stage from here," Keanan said.

The lawn-stage was set with bushes as props under the lights. Tall palm trees provided a skyline for a backdrop. The fluttering sounds of palm fronds high in the wind simulated a jittery audience in the high rafters, anticipating a performance. Here and there, a few lavish pines with low hanging boughs reached down and felt the ground, rubbing the grass nervously. Keanan thought he heard voices in their direction.

Then, as if on cue, actors began to appear from the shadows. An elegant group had begun stepping onto the stage from the wings. Chance and Keanan watched the players' entrance unfold. Keanan felt a shiver.

"What the hell …?" Chance craned his neck out from under the shadows for a better look.

Keanan began to worry. He had heard horror stories of people who had panicked and lost their minds. He intended to keep things light. He wondered if the gazebo were taking note.

"Are you seeing what I'm seeing?" Chance wore an alarming grin, while Keanan was yet adjusting his perspective.

Out of nowhere, a party of finely attired gentry had come to gather under the lights. Chance and Keanan could hear giggling from the silhouetted figures on the grass. There were wisps of perfume and flashes of jewelry. The hush of satin mixed with whispering pines in the breeze.

The spontaneous exhibition confused Keanan's ordinary sensibilities. *Is this for real?* He wasn't sure. Perhaps it was a private party of posh locals. *Maybe they're just out for some air by the ocean, the same as me and Chance.*

"They really look dressed up, don't they?" Keanan found his voice.

"Hell *yeah*, they do," Chance said.

The figures on the lawn looked as though they'd come from a grand gala, all of them dressed impeccably. The men boasted tuxedos with tails and the women wore long gowns and gloves, with dazzling tiaras and jewelry. The lights flooded in from behind them and their forms seemed to float as though in dance. Keanan and Chance gaped from the gazebo, mesmerized by the cotillion. Their visit had turned into a play. From their private box, they took-in the entertainment, which had snuck up on them as though a dream.

"This is crazy!" Keanan said.

"It's friggin' wild!" said Chance. "What the hell are they doing?"

"I have no idea."

On stage, one of the participants produced a balloon from his pocket and began blowing it up. Soon, another player followed and began blowing up another balloon too.

The first balloon was pink and the second, green. Several more balloons followed. All of them were long and thin, in multiple colors, the type clowns tie into shapes, but instead of twisting them into hats and animals, they allowed the balloons to remain long and straight, like skinny, pastel dirigibles. Their numbers continued growing.

"I can't believe I'm seeing this," Keanan said.

"It's weird. It's like the kind of crazy shit people at the museum would do," Chance said.

The elegant balloon blowers began attaching strings to their colorful airships and linking them all together. Their fleet of slender blimps aloft in the lights became a giant illuminated grid, expanding and growing nearer to where Keanan and Chance were sitting.

While Chance laughed at Keanan as he giggled like a kid, something new caught Chance's attention and he turned back toward the lawn.

"What's that over there, Kean?" Chance pointed.

Keanan squinted through the floodlights and thought he saw a clown—*a clown*—standing in the grass.

"That's funny," Keanan said.

"What, Kean?" Chance grinned at Keanan. "Do you see it?"

Keanan knew what it appeared to be, but he wasn't sure if he was actually seeing it. "It looks like a clown," he said. He began to laugh. The clown, in fact, looked familiar. He had seen one like it as a child. "This is *nuts*."

"Did you say a *clown*?" Chance was laughing too.

"They used to call him Jocko," Keanan said.

"Jocko."

It was Jocko the clown on the lawn, with his bald white head and diamond-shaped eyes—the one Keanan had seen as a boy at the circus. He remembered the baggy polka dot costume with the big round hoop inside.

"Yes! It's Jocko!" It made Keanan happy to see him again.

"Look again," Chance said.

Keanan followed Chance's eyes back to the lawn again. Another clown had come on stage and was standing with Jocko. This one had red hair and a yellow clown costume with an oversized tie in blue. Keanan admired his giant brown shoes.

"What are you seeing, Kean?" Chance said.

Keanan knew what he *thought* he saw, but again he wasn't sure. He tried turning the tables on Chance.

"Don't you see it?" Keanan asked. "What do *you* see?"

"I asked you first," Chance said.

Keanan hesitated, again confused.

"Look! … right over there." Chance gestured toward the clowns again.

As Keanan looked, he saw three or four other new clowns. One of them had already begun blowing up balloons.

"They must be late to the party, huh?" Keanan said. He prayed Chance was seeing the clowns too.

Chance began laughing loudly. "Clowns?" he said. "Is that what you're seeing?"

Keanan stared toward the lawn.

"Of course, clowns!" Chance laughed even harder. "Can you believe this? I was just fucking with you to see if you were seeing them too!"

"I knew it." Keenan smiled, relieved. "So, this is where they come to practice."

"It looks like they're taking over the place," Chance said.

The clowns had begun moving toward the center of the stage while the cotillion folk had begun retreating. Limousines with drivers were waiting on the street as the ladies and gents retreated from the lawn, out of the lights. One of the women tripped on a clown's big shoe and landed flat in the grass, ungracefully burying herself under her inflated dress. In a snit, the young woman jumped to her feet and snatched the clown's nose from his face, tossing it under the low branches of one of the pines. The clown shrieked in horror and dove after his nose, getting a face full of pine needles as he reached for it. Recovering his nose, he re-attached it and frowned while the woman went running away. He honked a brass horn in reproach at the woman until she reached a car and gathered herself in. Keanan and Chance watched in tears as the clown rejoined the others and they all resumed with their balloons.

Eventually, the thumping waves below the cliffs reminded Keanan and Chance there was a world beyond the circus. The clowns were losing their gusto and the balloons were becoming redundant. Keanan wondered if the gazebo had been keeping count. With the princes and princesses having driven away, the show appeared to be winding down.

"Well, I guess we should go." Keanan stood up from his gazebo wall seat.

"Yeah, we don't want to be the last ones at the party, huh?" Chance pulled his hood over his head.

They slipped away from their box and began walking away from the clowns instead of going back across the lawn. Moving along the edge of the bluffs, they glanced back every few yards. The beautiful balloon circus in the lights required several last looks. Soon, it would be gone and maybe never seen again. They needed to remind themselves it had actually happened.

"I'll bet if we look, we'll find a lady's shoe out there in the grass somewhere," Keanan said, which got Chance laughing again.

"Yeah, right," Chance said. "*Cinderella* ... ha, ha."

Following the path along the cliffs, they walked from the park until they reached the museum where Chance usually spent his working nights alone, guarding the exhibits. They stopped at the large structure and peered through a plate glass window.

"It gets scary in there, sometimes." Chance said.

"You're kidding." Keanan wanted to laugh.

"No. Seriously, it gets spooky in there!" Chance said. "I swear I hear things in this place at night. I *know* the place is haunted."

They continued walking around the building, peeking in the darkened windows. With only a few lights on inside, the dim statues and wall hangings appeared more like mausoleum trappings than art.

"Wasn't so bad, was it?" Chance said. The other windowpane— the one that had been in their drinks—was wearing off.

"I'm not saying a word," Keanan said. He would need to think it over later—all of it.

"The mushroom extract was kind of fun, don't you think?"

"I don't do that, man." Keanan said. "And, it wasn't mushrooms."

"You say." Chance said. He led Keanan around to the front of the building. Outside the entrance, he pointed through the glass to a telephone on a desk in the lobby. "That's where I call my girlfriend when the ghosts come out."

"Why am I not surprised?" Keanan said.

On the way back to the car, Keanan scanned the great lawn for shoes. Not finding any shoes or lingering clowns they got into Chance's car and went home.

Months later, when Chance suggested another windowpane trip, Keanan didn't offer any resistance, having well survived their circus night at the cove. Inspired by thoughts of the magical kingdom becoming even more magical, they looked forward to their new adventure with simmering excitement. The two friends each took a day off from work in the middle of the week, knowing Disneyland would be less crowded. It was spring, so it would be busy, but they kept thinking of how fun it would be to go on the fast rides and the Haunted Mansion. It would be especially wild while in their altered states of consciousness. Neither Curtis nor Keanan encouraged the other to rethink the ludicrous idea. The temptation was too great for either to think it through.

Chance and Keanan arrived at Disneyland early after an uneventful drive to Anaheim. The traffic had moved smoothly, but by the time they reached the Magic Kingdom at noon, the parking lot was already packed with cars. An attendant showed them to a parking space where they left Chance's car a quarter mile deep in the lot. A crowded tram took them to the main entrance.

It was not going to be another cool evening in a gazebo by the sea. Rather, the sunny day was Orange County hot—Southern California, developer-flattened, paved-over hot. Chance wore his favorite T-shirt, the one that had a large marijuana leaf emblazoned across the front. As soon as tickets were purchased, a gate attendant stopped them.

"Oh, sir! Wait!" The young man called Chance, but he was already through the turnstile. "You can't dress like that in here!"

Chance stopped in his tracks and spun around to face the attendant. His usual tack was sarcasm.

"Oh, WELL!" he said. "In *that* case, my mother thanks you, and my father thanks you! But I think I will just keep my clothes ON, if you don't mind!"

The attendant was stunned. Satisfied with himself, Chance turned around and began walking into the park.

"*Chance.*" Keanan grabbed Chance's shirt. "That's not what he means. You can't wear this shirt with the *bud* on it."

They had not come all the way to Anaheim just to turn around and drive back to San Diego. Fortunately, the problem was resolved easily. Chance had only to turn his shirt inside out and the attendant let them go.

The closest restroom was their first stop after the long drive. Then they bought sodas in plastic cups with straws and went back to the restroom again to drop a few windowpanes into their drinks. As they proceeded with their plan, the redundancy of it all occurred to Keenan for the first time. Disneyland was already a twisted realm of cartoons and princesses. He wasn't quite sure what was else was going to change. However, considering the harmlessness of the clowns and balloons at La Jolla Cove, he decided again to go along with Chance, just the same, while his better instincts failed to find a voice. Meanwhile, Chance, the seasoned day-tripper, didn't bother to count the number of little cardboard squares he dropped into their cups as they readied themselves for takeoff.

Having begun on foot in the magic kingdom, in five seconds they were airborne and in turbulence, making Keanan wish for a solid bench in a gazebo. Instead of gentrified dancers on the grass by the sea, the broad daylight forced upon them strollers stuffed with snot-nosed monsters, screaming and wielding plastic scimitars. There were aliens with huge heads running loose. Everywhere the creatures were chasing and attacking the throngs. Teen-aged grounds keepers in bright blue uniforms swept up trash as they leered like hungry wolves at the guests. Chance and Keanan felt they were being watched. Eyes were following as they walked cautiously to avoid scrutiny from the costumed roving bliss enforcers. The blinding day and the blur of movement had them craving shade and calm.

By the time Chance and Keanan reached the Haunted Mansion, they were primed for genuine horror. Once inside, as they stood in the cool foyer, the lights went out. Keanan felt himself swoon as the floor began dropping and the walls started growing taller. He knew they had made a drastic mistake.

"Oh, wow," Chance said. His anticipated mansion experience had begun.

"Yep ..." Keanan said, "... wow." He had to force his words. "This is really, really weird ..." It was all he could muster to say. That or scream in terror like everyone else, although the rest were all faking it.

Keanan was ready to drop on the floor, frothing at the mouth in fear, while Chance was merely becoming dull and catatonic. In the past, the lame haunted thrills had always disappointed Keanan. This time, his mind was on safety. Once the room stopped moving, Keanan and Chance followed others onto a platform, waiting to force themselves into one of the tin-can carts on a track. They stumbled into their seats and began moving again. As their wobbly shuttle took off, it spun around facing a mirror, reflecting another passenger, a skeleton, sitting in between them. Keanan was horrified. Then he saw what he thought was a dark figure hanging on to the outside of their cart, peering in at them, leering. It was so dark he couldn't tell whether his eyes were open or closed as the ride went on. Reality and Disney blurred. The agonizing haunting seemed to go on for hours. Yet, by the time the harrowing ordeal was over, their day was only beginning.

Once outside in the daylight again, Chance and Keanan realized they were not in synch with the rest of the denizens of Main Street. In their states, they had no peers among the tourists or the creatures with big heads.

"That wasn't so fun," Keanan said. He squinted hard in the sunlight, shading his eyes with his hand.

"What the hell happened in there?" Chance said. He was dizzy. "What did they *do* to that place?"

Keanan shook his head. "I think we should get the hell out of Dodge, don't you?"

"I say *screw* Disneyland, man!"

Chance's shouting surprised a few nearby guests as well as Mickey Mouse himself, only a yard away, who had been savagely patting the head of a sticky tot. Unfortunately, Chance's crude exclamation had offended the rodent in red shorts. Keanan could almost see scorn in the happy mouse's face as he turned his huge head toward Chance, smiling.

"What the hell you lookin' at, big ears?" Chance said.

"*Jeez*, Chance …" Keanan tried to quiet him.

What happened next was quick. Goofy came bounding out of nowhere, flopping tongue and tail, and Chance and Keanan were given a brisk escort to see-ya-later land. Goofy and Mickey knew of a secret hidden passage used for peculiar guests. In addition to posing with terrified tots, the big cartoon heads had subtle procedures for tossing out unruly patrons.

Poof! Chance and Keanan were out.

In mere seconds, they were standing outside of the park, in the sprawling parking lot again. Goofy had been gruff but polite in their departure, even inviting them to return in the future.

"Oh, yeah? Well, up yours too, Goofy!" Chance was cross and offended after being put out by a big dog. Only an hour had passed since they had gotten in, yet they were already finished at the happiest place on earth. The mouse had actually done them a favor, though. They wouldn't have dared get on another ride after their experience at the torturous mansion, but it was still of no consolation to Chance.

"Well, that was a big friggin' waste of money," he said.

Keanan was more embarrassed than angry and still coping with being high. "I'm still feeling this stuff, Chance. I think you put too much in our drinks this time."

"Look at this!" Chance said. He gestured toward the parking lot as if seeing it for the first time.

"Now what?" Keanan said.

They were back on the sweltering tarmac crammed with parked cars. The lot seemed spread out for miles. The only shadows were those cast by the monorail track weaving above the park. Keanan wished they were standing in some shade under the track or next to one of its tall trestle legs.

"Uh, oh ..." Chance muttered.

"What's the matter now?"

"I don't remember where the car is." Chance's mouth was gaping, his lips dry, and his eyes had a vacant look.

"You're kidding ... tell me you're kidding." Keanan said. He couldn't recall where they had parked car the car, either. "Start leading, Moses. You better find it."

"This sucks."

They started down one of the hundreds of rows. Chance's car was a bland, tan sedan that looked like an unmarked police car. It was going to be difficult to find. Keanan was growing concerned about the zombie expression on Chance's face. Maybe Chance was just thirsty. There was bottled water inside the car. They would need to find it soon, before Chance passed out or went for blood.

After wandering in the heat several minutes, Keanan was becoming tired and fed up. Following Chance was not getting them anywhere. He decided to tap into his own, uncanny sense-of-direction, which only seemed to kick in at times of desperate need.

"It's this way," Keanan said. He motioned Chance to follow.

"Whatever you say, governor."

Chance wandered behind as they trudged toward one of the tall support columns of the monorail track. Keanan nagged Chance to keep up. Soon, with his mental GPS having zeroed in on their target, Keanan rounded the back of a VW camper and found Chance's car, blessedly parked in a shadow.

"You saved us, Kean!" Chance startled Kean. They got inside the car laughing, and then began blasting the air conditioning and sucking down bottled water. After running the engine and cooling down for a few minutes, Keanan was still concerned about Chance.

"Are you okay to drive?"

"I'm fine, Jocko. Keep your nose on." Chance appeared pallid.

Keanan was too tired to laugh or argue.

Chance backed the car out of the space and began navigating the parking lot like a lost rat in a maze. Keanan feared Chance might begin bouncing off parked vehicles, driving in his hazy state. Chance then drove them out to an open area of the blacktop and began puttering in wide circles.

"I don't think this is what we should be doing, Chance," Keanan said. Chance found that driving in circles was fine as long as they were both enjoying the air conditioning. Keanan reached over and turned off the fan, hoping it would bring Chance back to the living.

Eventually, the magic of Disneyland touched them again—even in the parking lot of lost hopes, this time. Nothing escapes the big mouse's over-sized eyes and ears. After five minutes of doing circles in parking land, a plain-clothed escort in a golf cart came to lead them out. After exchanging pleasantries at the car window, Chance somehow managed to follow the little vehicle to an exit on Katella Avenue. It was just one very small leg on a long, mystical trip home.

Once in traffic, Chance did his best to keep straight—resisting any temptation to do loops. He concentrated intently on his driving, although neither Keanan nor Chance had any idea where they were heading. After a few long stoplights they happened upon an onramp to the 5-South freeway—Chance's runway to flight.

"Wow, that was lucky, huh?" Keanan said.

"Yeah?" Chance said. He was focused on the task ahead.

When the light turned green, cleared for takeoff, Chance gave it full gas heading up the onramp. Soon, they were soaring down the freeway—*actually flying in Chance's mind*. Chance truly believed the car was in the air, above the rest of the traffic. Unfortunately, Keanan had failed to realize Chance's lack of driving readiness before leaving Disneyland. Already in the air, it was too late for second-guessing. The cabin was pressurized.

Interstate-5 was crowded and fast, although Chance's car was still passing the rest. Pushing the accelerator, he also cranked up the radio and pressed the buttons to open all the windows. Freeway noise filled the car as they careened down the grooved white lanes. Chance's face had a vacant look as Keanan watched him drive. Further messing with their minds, the song, "Thriller," came over the radio.

"Can you hear that?" Chance was grinning.

"Hear what? The song?"

"No! ... That other sound! ... The helicopter!"

"What are you talking about?"

"Chopper!" Chance shouted. "Can't you hear the big blades? It's so loud!"

"All I hear is Michael Jackson," Keanan said. He reached and turned off the radio. Then he heard the sound Chance had described. It was a loud, rhythmic thumping like the sound of a large military helicopter.

"Now I'm hearing it too!" Keanan said. He was shouting and confused. "It sounds like a Coast Guard helicopter!"

"No, man! It's 'Nam! We got a troop carrier bird!"

"Vietnam? Like in the movies?"

"Wow, this sucker is quick!" Chance was on a mission.

Keanan believed they had both lost their minds. *Vietnam chopper?* He imagined hearing sad music, "Adagio for Strings." It was orchestrating their doom, playing in his head along with the sound of rotor blades. He could hear wailing violins and cellos, and the sounds of weapon fire. They were chasing over a war-ravaged jungle in a helicopter. He began wishing he were back with the freaks in Disneyland.

The car lurched hard to the right across three lanes. Then it swerved back two lanes as Chance dodged enemy fire. Keanan stiffened, terrified. Chance turned again to avoid more fire from the jungle below, nearly sideswiping a car. Again, their car careened wildly. They swept across four lanes to the left and back four lanes to the right, narrowly missing more traffic. Keanan looked at Chance and realized how horribly real it was that Chance believed he was flying a helicopter. He felt helpless looking at his friend's desperate expression. He wanted to yell at Chance to stop, but was utterly powerless. He could barely watch as they barreled on at high speed.

The frenzied maneuvers continued with Chance finessing like a veteran pilot. Their helicopter lurched to the right and nearly smashed into the wheels of a long, flatbed truck. Keanan stared in fear as they traveled alongside the vehicle carrying a huge load of timber. There was a gaping space underneath the truck's bed, and he had a clean view of the road speeding below it in a blur. As they moved just ahead of the carrier's rear wheels, Keanan was afraid Chance would try to cut through beneath it. Looking up from his window, he could see bulky metal chains holding down the load of massive tree trunks just inches above their car. He could smell the fresh cut logs. He then realized it was the lumber making the helicopter sounds. The stiff suspension of the trailer was making the logs jump. Even tethered with heavy chains, the load hopped in the trailer bed, thumping and creating sounds resembling that of heavy churning rotor blades. As the freeway wind blasted through the car, the effect was complete. Keanan was going to die in a helicopter crash and no one would ever know of it.

All at once, their car pulled away again. Keanan watched the freeway lanes open quickly between the overloaded truck and them. Cars were honking all around as Chance evaded enemy fire. They lurched and swerved, again heading toward the rumbling truck. Keanan was certain they were going to be swallowed underneath it this time. The truck's horn blasted, but Chance didn't hear it. He was too focused, too busy piloting the helicopter over the jungle. Keanan covered his head with his arms and closed his eyes, hoping for a miracle. He began to pray.

In the end, not even a speeding ticket came of it. Keanan and Chance emerged from their genuine horror ride unscathed. No magical Disney minions had saved them on the freeway, although at some point Keanan thought he had heard dogs barking. Somehow, they had made it back to San Diego alive and unhurt. It was plainly a miracle. Keanan had never been more grateful to be exiting a California freeway.

Keanan had recently rented a new apartment. He had moved from the one he had been sharing with Chance after finding a flat closer to his office that was only a few blocks from the freeway. They decided to go there directly and drove up the steep, short road to Keanan's apartment high in Mission Hills. His broad view looked west over the airport and the bay.

"Did I miss the airport?" Chance was looking out from where he had parked on the hillside lot.

Keanan shook his head and got out of the car.

It was a relief to be standing on firm ground. They paused for a moment to enjoy the breeze and the view, and then went inside to try to unwind.

Keanan's small bungalow was barely larger than the gazebo but he had managed to fit in a sofa bed, a chair, and an extravagant new audio system. He went to turn on some calming music, but was overwhelmed by his complicated system.

"What the hell you got in there?" Chance said. He hadn't seen Keanan's new toys. The smoked-glass-enclosed rack of electronic components was tall and imposing, but the dance club sized speakers in the tiny apartment were insane. "What are these? 16-inch woofers?" Chance began laughing. "You're crazier than I am!" He nosed over all the switches and unfamiliar controls, snickering but not touching anything.

"Yeah, well …" Keanan said, "I couldn't resist." His cottage didn't share any common walls, so he could get away with the extra wattage.

"What's with all these red buttons?"

"Thirty-two band graphic equalizer."

"Whoa," Chance said. "Who runs it for you?"

Staring at all the knobs and controls, Keanan realized he wasn't yet familiar with his new system, either. In fact, he was baffled by it just then. After finding the power switch and turning it on, he was too tired and confused to figure it out. He and Chance had no choice but to listen to classical music at an elevated volume.

Chance flopped on the floor and slept. Keanan meanwhile fumbled with the stereo. Unable even to turn it off, he lay on the sofa, still nervous from the flight home and desperate to relax. "Adagio for Strings" came on the radio—the last song he had expected to hear. Not able to stop the sad music, he resigned not to fight it and fell-in with the tragic adagio, this time. He became absorbed in the realism of the sounds coming from his speakers. The bass and contrabass came alive in the room. Every sad, sighing breath of the music was felt, reminding Keanan of the long drive home, thinking he was going to die in an imagined helicopter somewhere in Vietnam. Every edgy note of the violins screamed in his ears during a long, climactic crescendo. Then, as the music died down, he could hear the coughs and sniffles of the musicians in the orchestra captured on the recording. The basses resumed softly droning again, and the conductor turned more pages of his score. Fascinating and somber, the music continued until Keanan, too, finally slept.

Months after their mad chopper ride, Chance and Keanan

met for coffee near the cove. The summer sun was out, so they took their cups to the park by the ocean.

"This coffee sucks!" Chance said.

"Well, don't drink it then." Keanan's coffee was fine.

They went to the gazebo to sit and watch the tourists who were all looking toward the sea as they walked past, but not even noticing the gazebo.

"Did you hear about that guy that drowned?" Chance asked.

"Yeah."

A snorkeler who had been struggling in a heavy current was rescued by a surfer. The snorkeler had survived while the surfer had died in the rough water.

"He got caught in one of the caves just when the tide was coming in," Chance said.

"Yeah, I heard. He was a surfer, right?"

"Yeah … he should have known better, poor guy."

Keanan could sense the gazebo was listening as they sat in its shade. He traced with his finger one of the carvings in a weathered board.

"People do stupid things, don't they Chance?"

"They sure do, man," Chance said.

Keanan felt the gazebo holding its breath while Chance continued.

"Stupid people," Chance said. "What the hell were they doing down there, anyway? Taking chances like that …"

Keanan took a sip from his paper coffee cup and gazed across the great lawn.

"Wouldn't it be funny if this old gazebo could talk?"

Decision Thinking

THE FLASHING RED LIGHT was the first thing Jason saw when he opened his eyes. His Portable Decision Maker, or PDM, was telling him to recharge it. It was designed to make *that* decision too. However, this morning it had not awakened him with music as it usually did.

I must have forgotten to plug it in, Jason thought. Just before he had gone to bed, the PDM's small display had read: RECHARGE NOW.

Crap.

Not a big deal. It wouldn't ruin Jason's day. It wasn't in his nature to become stressed over little things.

"Are you up, Jason?" His father knocked on his bedroom door. They had been sharing the apartment ever since Jason's mother had passed. The arrangement was ideal under the circumstances. Father and son had been inseparable friends from the moment Jason was born.

"I'm good, Dad! … I'll be out in a minute."

Theirs was an enviable father-son relationship—always trusting, comfortable with affection, and with each of them mindful and respectful of his role in the other's life. Jason's father was overjoyed from the second he and his wife knew they were expecting a child. He had never stopped smiling from that moment. Ever since the boy's birth, Jason had been his father's steadfast source of joy. The giddy father swore the first thing his son did at birth was to smile at him. He liked to proclaim that his son, instead of crying when the doctor smacked his bottom, had merely laughed and looked over at his dad, smiling—as if to say hello!

"Okay, son!" Jason's father said. "I'm heading out to the station." He gave another tap on the door. "Have a good day, Jase!"

"Thanks, Dad. You too."

Jason would swear he remembered his own birth the same way as his father had. Their souls had connected when they saw each other for the first time. He had somehow known he and his father would be great friends for life. Not even the doctor's slap had stopped Jason from proceeding straight into laughing with his dad for the first time while the doctor still had him dangling by his feet.

Rolling over in his bed, Jason sat up. He reached for his PDM and plugged it into the wall socket. The device needed only ten seconds to charge. As he strapped it to his wrist, its small display monitor advised him his toe nails were due for clipping.

With his PDM charged and fully functioning, Jason strode to the kitchen in his pajama shorts to heat up some coffee. His PDM monitored his movements continuously—tracking his location, the exact time, and his proximity to nearby objects.

Beep.

Jason looked at his wrist and read the display.

Microwave Coffee 60 Seconds.

The monitor was easy to read. Its letters were clear and the messages concise. There was also an audible cue delivered via a custom chip, which had been painlessly implanted near his ear. The signal could be adjusted and customized to need, with only Jason hearing its alert at times when decisions were critical.

It was routine for Jason to glance at his PDM without

thinking. If not for its cues, he would otherwise have to make decisions for himself about things he didn't wish to have cluttering his mind—things that would detract from his memorizing the names and song titles of his latest music downloads. His PDM was a reliable reminder and kept his thinking on a sensible track during daily activities. It reduced mental effort and strain.

While Jason was starting his morning routine, his father came rushing back to the apartment.

"Forgot my badge," he said. "Getting a late start, son?" He grabbed his City Transit ID from the kitchen table and clipped it to his shirt pocket.

"Nah, I've got plenty of time," Jason said. He glanced at his wrist.

"Did that thing tell you I was coming back?" His dad was laughing at his PDM.

"No, but if you get one yourself, maybe you won't forget your ID all the time." Jason sniggered.

"Right." His dad winked.

As his father left the apartment again, Jason removed the filter from the coffee maker.

"See ya, Dad! Be careful!"

"Bye, son!"

Jason had brewed his coffee the night before to streamline his morning routine. He tossed the old filter in the trash, poured some cold coffee from the pot into a cup, and proceeded to re-heat it in the microwave for exactly 60 seconds as directed by his PDM—which also reminded him not to burn his mouth.

CAUTION. MICROWAVE COFFEE HOT.

Jason was a health-conscious man. He pampered his well-exercised body. It complemented his appealing face and smooth complexion. His vibrant appearance was admired on elevators, subways, and at the office. Jason enjoyed being noticed.

WAIT. BREAKFAST AFTER SHOWER.

Jason could burn off stored energy from the previous night's meal by waiting to eat until after he had showered. On the way to his shower, he removed and folded his pajama shorts before placing them on the end of his bed. In the bathroom, he let his undershorts drop to his feet. He then picked them up with the toes of his right foot, and deftly deposited them into the clothes hamper without losing his balance. He glanced at his wrist again.

TURN TAP IN TUB TO HOTTEST. ADJUST TO LUKEWARM.

Water at body temperature is best for the skin.

COMB.

Jason used his comb in the shower to apply his high-end hair conditioner. He saved money by using smaller amounts of the expensive product and combing it through his thick hair. The results were better coverage and more economical use of his preferred hair product.

STEP INTO MAT. DRAW CURTAIN. STEP BACK AFTER PULLING STOP.

As the water surged through the hose to the shower head, Jason stepped back to avoid the first splashes of cold water. He glanced at his PDM and wondered how it always stayed fog free, even with warm water washing over it. *When I was a kid, the earlier model always fogged up. I used to get in trouble for forgetting to wash my hair.*

As he marveled at the readability of his PDM, the device reminded Jason to stay on the non-slip mat. He rarely took baths, preferring instead to stand while directing the spray of the hand-held shower head.

SHAMPOO, RINSE.

Following the prompts, the morning routine progressed.

THREE PUMPS CONDITIONER. COMB THROUGH HAIR.

Jason combed the conditioner through his hair, leaving it on while he shaved.

AVOID FINGERS, NOSE, LIPS. KEEP RAZOR FLAT AGAINST SKIN. USE CAUTION ON NECK.

After shaving and brushing his teeth, Jason lathered up with skin-conditioning soap, and then scrubbed himself vigorously for one minute. Finally, he rinsed off with the shower head on high, sprayed down the shower, and turned off the tap. Looking at his wrist again, he would have forgotten one critical step if not for the reminder.

Take comb.

Once, when Jason hadn't worn his PDM, he had left his comb in the shower when he had finished, and had lost several seconds searching for it. By the time he found it, he was already behind schedule and needed to rush while readying for work.

Today, Jason's PDM was holding its charge well, thanks to a recently replaced the battery. It prodded him promptly during every step of his regimen while he prepared to leave for work.

How did people manage without a PDM way back when? It seemed a fair question to Jason, even though his father had frequently tried to tell him that to function in life effectively, one needed to have common sense—*whatever that meant.* Jason's father had told him such traits were not inborn and had to be learned.

Moisturize while skin is damp.

After patting dry with a clean towel, Jason stepped from the tub and squeezed a generous amount of hypoallergenic moisturizer onto his hands. He lavished the cream over his body quickly to lock in the moisture from his shower.

Eyes. Smooth downward, inward.

He dabbed on a small amount of eye cream and massaged it in gently, using a light circular motion. Jason always followed directions well.

After applying three additional creams and emollients as directed by his PDM, Jason completed his routine by spraying his armpits with antiperspirant.

Avoid cutting toenails too close.

Thanks. I probably would have aggravated my big toe again. It took another couple of minutes for Jason to clip his toenails with precision. *Nice job.*

Putting on clean underwear and selecting a shirt, Jason

finished getting dressed. He pulled on his slacks, buckled his belt and attached his portable music device. He could hardly wait to listen to the latest music he had downloaded the night before. He glanced at his wrist.

BREAKFAST: YOGURT. NO ADDL. CARBOHYDRATES. TAKE VITAMINS.

Jason helped himself to a small plastic cup of yogurt from the refrigerator. Between spoonfuls, he sorted out a dozen vitamin supplements, which he took daily, consulting his PDM while selecting various tablets and capsules. He finished his morning coffee, washing down the vitamins.

YOGURT CUP. SPOON. COFFEE CUP. POT.

The yogurt cup went into the recyclables. The spoon, he placed in the dishwasher along with his coffee cup. He finished his routine by rinsing out the coffee pot and leaving it on a rack by the sink.

His PDM vibrated for the first time that morning, tickling his wrist while alerting him to a personal message, which scrolled across the small screen.

CHERYL: "HI. HOPE YOU HAVE A WONDERFUL DAY! I'M OFF TO WORK."

She must have been in a hurry. It was the same message Cheryl's PDM usually sent out when she was running late. He would catch up with her later, after work.

Jason left the apartment listening to his music player. It was a short walk to the busy transit station and then a quick two-stop subway ride to his downtown office. He enjoyed a passion for digitized Trance music. He found it elevated his senses during his commute. The incongruous, ethereal sounds and the sizzling rhythms of the music gave him a sense of escape from his otherwise ordinary life. He could imagine he lived in an avant-garde, futuristic world as he observed other commuters while the seething, techno-music riffs swirled in his head. His PDM would occasionally beep loudly through his ear chip to keep him from getting on the wrong escalator or using the wrong stairs while traversing the station. In his usual form, Jason arrived at work on time, having enjoyed another surrealistic ride underground and the short walk to his office building—all the while happy in his own little techno world.

Jason's job at a corporate conglomerate was in customer service handling retail product issues over the telephone. Once at work, his PDM automatically linked with his employer's software and converted its processes to a work related decision-making function. While conversing with customers, Jason would glance at his wrist for cues as he listened.

"I can't believe this piece of crap you sent me!" His first customer complained as Jason listened on his head set. "How do you people get away with selling this junk and charging so much for it?"

Jason looked at his PDM and read the cue.

MAKE MONETARY ADJUSTMENT FOR CUSTOMER. [COST FOR REPEAT CALLS AND FUTURE ADJUSTMENT HIGHER THAN CUSTOMER PAID PRICE.] DO NOT EXPLAIN COMPANY REASONS. APOLOGIZE.

When he had been in training, Jason had heard that his company's past procedure had been to challenge customers and argue until they hung up. The strategy was intended to discourage refunds, even when the company's product was bad or misrepresented. However, the company found that customers would usually call back and complain to someone else. Repeat customer calls were driving up staffing costs. Furthermore, newer inexperienced representatives were unlikely to negotiate effectively or make creative decisions. Thus, policy was changed and a new strategy was implemented—that of utilizing employees' own PDMs to affect company rule-sets and efficiently handle customer complaints.

"Are you listening to me?" Jason's customer was screeching at him in his headset. "I want my money back! And, I'm not paying to send this piece of garbage back to you, either!"

Jason followed a prompt from his PDM to read aloud from a script, which appeared on his desktop monitor.

"I am very sorry, sir," Jason said. He tried to sound sincere as he read from the script. "I will have a refund applied in your original form of payment, immediately. We apologize for any inconvenience."

How does the company even know it's cheaper just to cave in and refund in this case? Jason was only vaguely curious. He was not even sure which item the customer had purchased. He was actually glad not to have had all of that useless information cluttering up his brain. He would much rather work on memorizing song lyrics sung by his favorite new musical group. He glanced at his PDM.

REFUND AMOUNT: 472 EUROS.

Six hours later, having completed another successful work day, and having switched his PDM back to non-work mode, Jason went home and then adjusted his PDM to gym mode. He dressed for his daily workout.

NON-ELASTIC WAISTBAND SHORTS.

Jason didn't need the reminder. The change to looser shorts had already saved his lower back. His muscles used to seize up during exercise because of the tight elastic waistband of his former gym shorts. After he had bought a more comfortable pair, he had neglected to delete the old reminder. His PDM did not remind him to remove outdated reminders.

As Jason worked out in the well-equipped spa in his apartment building, his PDM regularly gave him useful cues and reminders:

NO SUDDEN BENDING ... AVOID PULLING BAR ONTO HEAD ... AVOID CRUSHING FINGERS ... KEEP EYES OPEN ... STOP AT 15 REPS ...

The PDM was especially active while at the gym, mainly to help prevent avoidable injuries during Jason's hour-long routines.

After finishing his workout in the basement gym, Jason chose to take the stairs to his fourth floor apartment instead of the elevator.

KEEP ONE HAND ON RAIL.

Once back in his apartment, Jason switched his PDM back to primary mode again.

SMOKED FISH. CRACKERS. TOMATOES. NON-FAT FROZEN YOGURT.

Dinner could wait for a few minutes while he focused on downloading some new songs to his music device.

"Is that you, Jason?" his father called from the living room. Jason's dad was relaxing in his favorite chair, watching the news on television.

"Yes, Dad. How was your day?"

"I'm good. There was a lot of traffic near the station. It was kind of crazy … as usual."

"Oh … yeah … Did you eat?"

"Yeah … had some leftover pizza from work and a couple of carrots … You good?"

"I'm fine, Dad … I'll just eat one of my healthy concoctions." Jason heard his dad chuckling in the living room.

Knowing that his dad was happy and fed, Jason could focus on his hobbies for a while before eating something himself. What mattered most to him was cataloging the names and titles of music artists in his mind and their latest edgy songs.

While in the midst of downloading his music, Jason's PDM interrupted him, vibrating on his wrist. He glanced at the display.

CHERYL: "HI. HOPE YOU HAD A WONDERFUL DAY! DOING ANYTHING?"

She's anxious for the weekend. Jason sat at his desk and scanned a stack of interactive games. Reaching for one, his eyes were drawn to his PDM again.

USE CAUTION. SMOKED FISH CONTAINER HAS SHARP METAL EDGES.

Three hours later, Jason ate his canned smoked fish on wheat crackers. He decided to skip the frozen yogurt. It was too late at night for the extra calories. He brushed his teeth and went to bed, listening to the music he had downloaded. He slept soundly throughout the night, unaware that another minor glitch in his PDM would be waiting for him in the morning.

CHARGE ERROR. SERVICE REQUIRED.

Waking on time, even without the benefit of an alarm, Jason noticed his PDM had malfunctioned. With dull concern, he got out of bed and left the PDM in its charger.

It's probably something minor. No big deal.

Standing in the bathroom, Jason tried to remember whether he had eaten breakfast. He glanced at his wrist, but his PDM wasn't there. He would need to drop it off for repair on his way to work.

I need some coffee.

As his coffee heated in the microwave for 90 seconds, Jason doled out his daily vitamins into a small ceramic container. He admired the crackled finish of the little jade colored bowl as he dropped various colored capsules and tablets into it.

Removing his cup from the microwave and holding it to his mouth, the boiling liquid scalded his lips and burned his tongue.

"Ah!" Jason dropped the cup. The mug fragmented on the floor at his feet and hot liquid splashed on his toes. "*Fuck!*" He yelled and danced on the floor, shaking his stinging feet.

Ouch! ... Hell! ... I don't have time for this!

The burns were not serious, but Jason's tongue still hurt as he finished picking up the broken pieces of his cup and mopping the kitchen floor. He spent a few more confused minutes wiping down splashed appliances and cabinets. Out of habit, he glanced at his wrist ... nothing.

Do I want some yogurt?

Now running late, Jason moved on to the bathroom and stepped into the shower. He bent and turned on the tap. A shock of cold water from the shower sprayed his head and back.

"Ugh!" He quickly reached for the shower knob and adjusted the water.

Fuck! … Why does it do that?

He could feel his back muscles seizing-up as he bent. Adjusting the water warmer, he stood up in pain and tried to let his back relax. As the water ran through his hair, he glanced down at his wrist again. No PDM.

Feeling the light stubble on his chin with his fingers, Jason stared into his shaving mirror and slathered gel onto his face. As he made a first pass with his shaver, he was horrified as blood began flowing down the side of his face, mixing with the shower water and dribbling down his chin and neck. The razor had painlessly cut a neat slice on his right nostril.

What the hell? My face! My beautiful nose! What the fuck did I do?

Jason tried to calm himself and make his anger go away. He could usually blow off the small things easily.

Stupid razor!

Finishing his shower and then staining his white towel with blood, Jason stared at his face in the mirror as the side of his nose bled for another minute. After holding several Kleenexes in place, the bleeding eventually stopped. By then, Jason had an urgent need to pee and was running late. Glancing at his wrist, there were still no hints as to what to do next.

Overlapping to save time, Jason grabbed his blow dryer and stood in front of the toilet urinating as he switched it on. The lights went out and the dryer stopped. With his strong stream still flowing, Jason turned in the dark, spraying the walls, the towels, and the floor while the blow dryer slipped from his hand and into the toilet. He couldn't stop what he had started, regardless of where it was going, but managed to unplug the dryer and fish it out of the toilet once he was done. After restoring the lights, he assessed the damages.

That could have turned out a lot worse. He put the wet blow dryer on top of the pile of red-spotted tissues in the waste basket.

The sight of all the blood made him feel dizzy. He glanced at his wrist again. Nothing.

Did I eat breakfast?

Back in the kitchen, Jason stepped on a shard from his broken coffee cup. It made a painful cut in the bottom of his foot and was difficult to find. He was able to tweeze it out, but then followed up by dotting the kitchen floor with a new batch of blood spots while looking for yogurt and a spoon for his late breakfast. He glanced at his empty wrist again and noticed his vitamins still on the counter where he had left them in the little jade bowl.

Running behind, Jason dressed quickly, wearing the same shirt he had worn the day before, his work identification card still in the breast pocket. He then dashed out of his apartment and waited in the hallway for the elevator. He knew he could still be on time for his subway if the elevator came quickly. He hoped for even a slight change of luck. After only a few seconds, the elevator door opened and Jason stepped inside, glancing at his wrist. Nothing. He realized he had forgotten his PDM and he urgently needed to drop it off for repairs. Knowing the matter couldn't wait, he jumped out of the elevator just before the doors closed and ran back to his apartment to retrieve the malfunctioning device.

After retrieving his PDM and running down his building's stairs to the street, Jason hurried the few blocks to the subway station. Along the way, the traffic in the street appeared jammed for several blocks, apparently due to a stalled bus. While walking fast to catch his subway downtown, Jason still managed to enjoy his music player and get to the station quickly without incident.

As he listened to his music, recalling the artists and titles he had memorized the night before, Jason's public transit card, still in his pocket, automatically cleared his way at each turnstile, allowing him to continue uninterrupted. The subway ride was uneventful except for a trickle of blood from the side of Jason's nose, most of it drying on his cheek. Only a few drops managed to reach his shirt before the bleeding stopped again. He hadn't heard the woman standing above him mention he was bleeding. As the doors of the subway opened at his destination, Jason moved with the other passengers toward the escalators leading to the station exits. Glancing at his wrist, and seeing his PDM not there, he remembered it was in his pocket and he needed to drop it off for repair.

Near the bottom of the escalators was a small PDM shop. Jason quickly dropped off his device and moved on. If his PDM had been working just then, he would have noticed another cheerful message from his girlfriend. Instead, the PDM technician, with Jason's device in hand, was smiling as he read it.

CHERYL: "HI. HOPE U HAVE A WONDERFUL DAY! I'M OFF TO WORK."

Jason never saw the message. Gripping the rubber railing of the escalator, Jason steadied himself as he neared street level. His foot caught the grooved metal at the top and he tripped and stumbled forward. Catching himself before doing a face plant on the pavement, he managed to avoid a bad landing, only scraping and dirtying his hands. *No big deal.* Always the optimist, he picked himself up and continued toward the street. He could see the clock in the lobby of his building on the other side of the intersection. It appeared he still had a few minutes to spare. *At least I made it to work on time.* He dusted off his hands as he walked quickly.

In the busy street, a bus came rushing to pick up passengers. It was the bus that had stalled at another station. It had caused such a backup that large crowds of passengers were now standing around waiting at a nearby curbside stop. Ignoring the crowds, Jason looked down at his music player and adjusted the volume as he stepped off the curb to cross the street.

In the repair shop at the base of the escalator, the man diagnosing Jason's PDM was again amused by another odd message in its display. Although the device was unable to transmit an audible signal to the implant next to Jason's ear, the device still displayed its simple common sense warning:

LOOK BOTH WAYS BEFORE CROSSING THE STREET.

Jason stepped directly in the path of the oncoming bus and was hit hard. He became airborne and landed several yards away under a bus stop bench. Crowds of waiting passengers had just begun herding toward the approaching bus when Jason went flying past them. The bus shuddered to a halt, the station echoing with the sound of its brakes, a baleful, groaning sound. The bus driver leapt from his seat, squeezed past frightened passengers, and pushed his way out the door and into the street. He ran from the bus and over to the fallen pedestrian who lay under the bus stop bench.

"Jason!" The driver recognized his son and winced. "*What were you doing?*"

Looking down at the young man laying silent on the cement with his eyes closed, the father touched his son's arm, noticing the PDM was missing from his boy's wrist.

"You're supposed to know this stuff, son." His voice was strained as he admonished his boy. "You're not supposed to need that stupid wrist watch to tell you not to walk in front of a bus." He cradled his son in his arms as he scolded him.

The crowd surrounded the bus driver, watching, but he didn't seem to notice them. He didn't care about the commotion on his bus where the passengers were gawking in his direction.

"Come on, boy!" he said. "… We're supposed to be friends, remember?" The crowd could feel his aching as he pleaded with Jason.

When Jason began to move in his arms, his father was reminded of his first meeting with his newborn son, when all they could do was smile at each other. This time, his son spoke.

"I remember, Dad," Jason said, opening his eyes. Upon seeing his dad's face, he burst into a grin and began laughing loudly while his dad joined in.

No one was seriously hurt. The incident was mentioned only briefly in the local news. The next day, while Jason lay in bed at home, recuperating from scrapes and bruises, the telephone rang and his father answered it in the living room.

"It's the repair shop, son!" His father held the phone to his chest. "They said your thingy is ready!"

Jason had to think for a moment.

"Tell them to keep it, Dad!" he shouted. "I don't want it back!"

He waited for his father's reply, but only heard chuckling.

"They can keep it, Dad!" Jason repeated.

"You sure?" His father responded.

"Yeah, I guess I've decided," Jason said. Hearing his father's laughing becoming louder in the other room, Jason began laughing too.

"Decided, he says," Jason's father said to himself. Then, speaking to the man on the telephone, "Keep it. ... My boy actually made a decision! ... Just keep it."